THORNS

by J.O. Thompson

Copyright © 2023 by J.O. Thompson

All rights reserved. No part of this book may be reproduced, stored in a retrieval system, or transmitted in any form or by any means—electronic, mechanical, photocopying, recording, or otherwise—without prior written permission of the publisher, except for brief quotations in critical articles or reviews.

Scripture quotations taken from the Holy Bible, New International Version®, NIV®. Copyright ©1973, 1978, 1984, 2011 by Biblica, Inc.™ Used by permission. All rights reserved worldwide.

First Edition

Cover design by J.O. Thompson

Then he told them many things in parables, saying: "A farmer went out to sow his seed. As he was scattering the seed, some fell along the path, and the birds came and ate it up. Some fell on rocky places, where it did not have much soil. It sprang up quickly, because the soil was shallow. But when the sun came up, the plants were scorched, and they withered because they had no root. Other seed fell among thorns, which grew up and choked the plants. Still other seed fell on good soil, where it produced a crop—a hundred, sixty or thirty times what was sown. Whoever has ears, let them hear."

"Listen then to what the parable of the sower means: When anyone hears the message about the kingdom and does not understand it, the evil one comes and snatches away what was sown in their heart. This is the seed sown along the path. The seed falling on rocky ground refers to someone who hears the word and at once receives it with joy. But since they have no root, they last only a short time. When trouble or persecution comes because of the word, they quickly fall away. The seed falling among the thorns refers to someone who hears the word, but the worries of this life and the deceitfulness of wealth choke the word, making it unfruitful. But the seed falling on good soil refers to someone who hears the word and understands it. This is the one who produces a crop, yielding a hundred, sixty or thirty times what was sown."

Matthew 13:3-9 & 18-23

PART ONE: SEED ALONG THE PATH

1

It was the worst sermon I had ever preached. Maybe the worst I'd ever heard. Quite possibly the worst sermon in the history of sermons. The Christian faith had just been set back one hundred years by the drivel I'd just spewed onto my congregation. I suppose the only consolation was half of them were asleep and the other half were looking at their phones or watches.

Bill Jones sat in his customary spot toward the rear left of the sanctuary. He had the decency to try and hide his mouth as he yawned. He was getting good at it. George Liston was not so polite and gaped openly and grunted when Lila, his wife, elbowed him in the ribs. It was the most excitement any of them had all morning.

I asked the congregation to bow their heads with me as I called for the closing prayer. Before starting in, I said my own little prayer that God would put the words in my mouth. That He would give His children something to leave with. Something from Him. But as it came out of my mouth and over the speaker system, I'm afraid all they got was my bumbling words. A horrible prayer. Uninspired. Maybe not as bad as the sermon, but the two seemed to go hand in hand.

***

The worship team started the closing song, and I exited the stage area and went out the back door, forcing myself to stand straight and hold my head up. I wanted to climb in my car and just head home, but I needed to get around to the front doors of the church to greet everyone as they left. Could you "greet" people if they were leaving? Made as much sense as the sermon had.

I stood outside the door and listened as the song came to a close. The late morning temperatures were just right. The sun was out and the day promised sunshine and barbeques. And allergies. Most of the trees were blooming and the temps seemed to send the pollen count into orbit. I could hear the muted sounds of shuffling and talking as people got up and gathered their coats and hats and such. I opened the door and put on my smiling face.

A guy I'd never seen before was the first to leave. His jeans were greasy and his shirt had a hole in it. His hair looked about a month from its last shampooing. I thanked him for coming and he grunted something while averting his eyes. I caught the aroma of alcohol and marijuana as he sped past, and I felt like I should pull him to the side and talk to him. Like this guy probably needed God's healing and peace right now. But after what I had just preached? He was probably already on a better track than what I had to offer today.

Luckily, Dave was the next one out. He gave me a quick embrace and headed straight for the greasy jeans guy. Thank God for good elders. Dave was the best, often helping me out, and certainly encouraging me when I needed it. I hoped he wasn't going to use all of his encouragement on the new guy, because I had enough to keep him busy.

The rest of the congregation filed out the door, some stopping to shake my hand or give me a hug. The majority went by the side, heading out for the rest of their Sunday. Maybe breakfast. Maybe some yard work. The ones that stopped perfunctorily thanked me or told me that I'd given a good sermon. I wanted to ask them if they could tell me what it was about, but that was unfair.

No sense taking out my frustrations with MY sermon on them. Besides, I already couldn't remember what it was about myself. Something about judging others... I don't know.

George and Lila Liston were towards the end. They had grabbed their son, Matthew, from the youth group. George glanced at his watch and touched Lila's back to hurry them along. Matthew wore his customary all-black shorts and hoodie. Earbuds in, of course.

"Great sermon, Pastor," George hollered with a half-smile. "Short and to the point. We can still catch the second half of the game."

Lila elbowed him again as they went down the steps.

Matthew lagged behind. "How was youth group, Matthew?" I asked.

He looked up at me and pulled one of the ear buds out. I could plainly hear some profanity laden "music" coming from the little device.

"Huh?"

I guess this whole place was inspiring. "Nothing," I said. "Have a good day."

He plugged back in and strolled over to his parents' car. Lila waved as they pulled away. I waved back, only getting my hand to chest level. Even my waves lacked energy.

Dave was still talking with the greasy jeans guy over in the shade of one of the trees in front of the church. He glanced my way and saw me looking, but gave me a small wave, letting me know he had it handled. That I wasn't needed over there either.

Mary came out with James. Mary and I had been married for fifteen years and she had dutifully followed me from church to church in the early years. But we'd been in Lamont now for eight years, a modicum of permanence had settled into our lives, which was a nice feeling for a young pastor. I liked to think I was still young. James had been born a few years before we moved here from Texas. He was our only child, though not for lack of trying.

He came running over to me and I bent down to scoop him up, burying my frustration within myself. "Hey, big man, how was Sunday School?"

"It was good, Dad. We got goldfish and brownies." The specks of chocolate in his teeth evidence of the mandatory Sunday School health program.

I set him back on the ground and gave Mary a kiss. I glanced down at James. "You have any time for the school part in between all of the snacks?" But he was already distracted, swinging from the steel handrail of the steps.

Mary put her arm around my waist. "How did things go today?" She wouldn't know, unless she had heard the snoring. She stayed in the back rooms, helping with the Sunday School program, though not with James's class. She helped with the high schoolers.

"Not the best," I said, stuffing my hands in my pockets. I gazed skyward, like there was something up there that needed my scrutiny. "The pastor wasn't on his A-game today."

"Oh, I'm sure it wasn't that bad," she said. But she must have seen something in my face. "You want to talk about it? I can drop James off at Mrs. Kirpatricks if you wanted to get some lunch."

I tried to buck it up for my wife. "No, its fine. We can talk about it tonight." I gave her the most reassuring smile I could muster. Besides, she and James always did something with just the two of them after church. They might go to the park or something like that as I usually had things to wrap up here.

"If you're sure," she said again as she gathered up James.

"Bye, Dad!" James yelled, as only a ten-year-old boy could.

THORNS

I left my hands in my pockets and shuffled to the back of the church and went through the rear door. My office sat behind the small kitchen that the church used on special occasions. I could hear the electric hum from the refrigerator unit running and the occasional drip from the kitchen sink. Another item on the list. I unlocked my office door and went in, plopping down into the chair behind my desk.

There were no messages or missed calls on my cell phone, but that wasn't unusual. I rapped my fingers on the desk for a while until that excitement passed. Then I spun around in my chair a couple of times. Looked at the books aligned on the wall.

I got up and stood right in front of my bookshelf. The odor of the pages entered my nostrils, reminding me of a library or a thrift store. I pulled one book out at random and blew the dust off the top, a small cloud catching the sunlight through the meager window I had. It was a rather large collection of books. Theological tomes and bible studies and how-to books on living the Christian life. Some had never done much for me, but some of them were inspiring. Pushed me to move or stretched the bounds of my thinking. But now, most of them just sat on the wall collecting dust. I thought of my congregation again and sighed.

Maybe I'd just go home. I could sit around and feel sorry for myself on the couch until Mary and James got home and then I could try to drag them down to my level. Not that I could drag Mary down. No sir. She would help me through it. She wouldn't emptily tell me that my sermon was good, but she wouldn't let me bask in my own pity either. God had done me a huge favor when he gave me Mary. Without Mary and James and Dave, I'd probably be sharing a room or an overpass with that greasy jean guy tonight.

Clearing off my desk a little, I came across my sermon notes from today. I pitched them in the trash under my desk and then fired up my computer. Maybe I should start on next week already. Work on an apology. Or a resignation letter.

A soft rap came from the door, and Dave came in. He took a seat across the desk from me.

"Hey, Bob," he said.

"Hi, Dave. You have a good talk with that guy out there?"

"Yeah, real good I think. He's been on the street for a while. A very sad story. I tried to encourage him a bit. Something got him in our door this morning. He's searching. Maybe he's seeking, and, if he is, then Jesus should find him."

"Yeah," I said.

We sat there a bit in silence. Not awkward. Dave and I were too good of friends for that.

He indicated my computer. "Hard at it already?"

I leaned back in my chair and it creaked as I put my hands behind my head. "No, I just turned it on in case you came by."

More silence. Dave picked up a book on my desk and looked at the title. Flipped through some of the pages, then set it back down and looked at me.

"How are you doing, Pastor?"

I sighed and took a deep breath. "I don't know, Dave. I'm just... I don't know. Down? Depressed? Discouraged?"

He arched an eyebrow. "Everything at home's good, right? James has to bring a smile to your face. That young boy energy."

Dave smiled to himself. He was like an uncle to James, and I knew James made him happy, too. But I also knew James cause him a bit of pain as well.

Dave had been going to Lamont Community Church for a long time. He was here well before I showed up. His wife Elena also used to be a regular attendee, back when they were young. They, too, had only one child. A child that they had tried and tried to have. That they wanted so deeply. At the time, they possessed an "if it's His will" attitude. But God had also taken that child, and it made that attitude hard to maintain.

I'd say, if anything, it perhaps strengthened Dave's faith. But if shattered Elenas. Their lives had been changed, including their marriage and their relationship with one another. Not broken or hateful, but … changed. Dave and I had spoken many times about it, especially when I was new here. I suppose I counseled him, but he counseled me just as much. He was my elder now, and we had a strong friendship. Maybe stronger for the hardships that we'd shared with one another.

"Yeah, good at home," I said. "Nothing like that. It's just in my head, I guess. Some sort of funk."

"Kind of like your sermon." Dave was a good elder: he didn't sugar coat things.

"It seemed a little painful," I agreed. "There had to be something good in there though, right?"

"Well, the guy I talked to said some of the things you said spoke to him. He cried a little even. Maybe it wasn't as bad as we're making out."

A little hope. "Anything speak to you?"

"I don't know. I forgot what it was about already." Good ole Dave. But it did make me laugh and laughter always seems to perk me up. At least a little. Dave chuckled too.

"Look," I said, "you got time for coffee later? I need to decompress a little, but maybe in an hour or so? Unless you're going fishing or something."

"No fishing today, Bob. I got time. I think Elena's out golfing. See you in a bit."

He shut the door behind him and the silence came back. I turned on the little radio I had tuned to a jazz station out of Bakersfield. I wasn't all that into jazz, but I needed a little background noise. Something with no lyrics.

I turned the computer back off. I wasn't going to do anything today. Not on the computer, at least. Besides, I already pretty much had a sermon in mind for next week. The next couple weeks, actually. Maybe six. I was going to present the parable of the soils to the congregation and we were going to divide the text into multiple weeks to see how we could cultivate our soil to be receptive to God's Word. It was a farming community: they would understand.

No, I thought maybe I would just sit here and reflect on things. It's not like people don't get into slumps. Even Christians. Even pastors. I knew the coffee time with Dave would help. And tonight with Mary would cheer me up. Wrestling with James on the floor always helped, too.

But right now I'd give myself a couple more minutes to wallow in it and then I'd work on getting out of this funk. Read a little in my Bible. Probably John, even if it was the only gospel not to include the parable I would be preaching on. Maybe a little prayer time to ask for direction. Just settle down a bit and refocus.

I pulled my old Bible off the shelf. New King James Version. Red cover that was all tattered and I opened it up to John. It was my favorite Bible, although I didn't really know why. I think I'd gotten it at a thrift store or something. Maybe because it had big letters. I flipped to John, but just couldn't get into it.

So, I decided I would just pray. I was going to lay this all out in front of the Lord and dump it on Him. I folded my hands and closed my eyes and started to pray as some saxophone solo went on in the background.

Father, I don't know what I've got going on in my head, but I do know that You've got it handled and figured out. I trust in Your holy plan and will. And You have given me so much, I feel bad for feeling bad, but I can't help it.

THORNS

Thank you, Lord, for the people You've placed in my life. Especially Mary. I don't know what I'd do without her. And Dave's dedication to Your church here. And to me. I would like to be a blessing to their lives. A blessing to the congregation.

But it's hard to do that when I feel like I'm slacking. Like I don't have anything worth saying. Lord, will you help me? Help Your church here? I go in front of them every week, but it's always just the same thing. The same people. And it doesn't feel like we're doing anything. Like we're not changing or living to be more like You.

Will this sermon next week change anything? Can we do anything about our soil? To get closer to You? To act like we believe what You say and that we could act as Christ would?

It's like we're just going through the motions. How can I get their attention, Lord? How can I get them to take this seriously? How can I make a difference? Your Spirit has to be here, right? Is it the people in the seats? Is it their pastor?

Jesus, I need help. I need You.

It was a good prayer. Heartfelt. Like a father wishes his kids would talk to him. I wish I could have given a prayer like that to the congregation. Sometimes the Spirit does indeed take over and you get such a cleansing feeling from prayer and from giving over your burdens to Christ.

I found that I was no longer in my chair. That I had ended up on my knees with my hands outstretched on the floor and my forehead on the ground.

I had tears running down my face.

There was a knocking at the door again. Dave must have forgotten something.

I stood up, my knees popping, and wiped my eyes and cleared my throat. I pulled my shirt down straight. "C'mon in, Dave."

The door opened, but it wasn't Dave.

2

Some guy I'd never seen before came into my office. He was medium height. A little skinny. He had dark curly hair, but cut fairly short. A large nose and goatee adorned his face and he wore jeans and a tee shirt. Normal guy. Clean. Darker skin, but not like the Hispanic people around Lamont. His features weren't delicate like a lot of Hispanics. More abrupt, with a deep brow. He looked a little familiar, but I didn't think I'd ever met him before. He maybe could have passed for the greasy jeans guy if the greasy jeans guy were to shower and get a haircut.

"How you doing?" I said. "I'm Pastor Bob Jordan. Something I can do for you?" I stuck out my hand and the guy shook it. Rough hands, like someone who built things. But not dirty. Friendly.

"Can we sit down?" the guy asked.

"Oh, yeah, sure. Please do." I sat behind my desk again and he took the chair that Dave had just vacated.

He wore a persistent smile. No teeth showing, but a content look. He settled his arms on the chair rests and looked at my books on the shelf and my degrees in frames. He did show some teeth when he glanced at the picture of Mary and James. Not creepy, though. He didn't seem to be in a hurry. I fought back the urge to look at my watch.

He looked at me like he'd read my mind. "Sorry," he said, "just checking out your office. Nice. Some good books you have."

"Thanks," I said. It was strange, for sure. But the guy seemed harmless. Maybe he was working up to whatever he wanted to talk about. Usually, members from the congregation would call me to set an appointment. Sometimes they came by in person, hoping to find me, not wanting to talk about their issues over the phone. Which was sound logic. In person was much better.

And it wasn't totally abnormal to have some stranger show up. They saw the church as a beacon of hope, which was good, and they often felt the pastor could help them through their issues. That maybe wasn't so good, but it seemed to come with the territory. I almost felt bad for this guy: he'd caught me on an off day. But I would certainly do what I could.

"So..." I started. "Something I can do for you? Something you want to talk about? This your first time here?"

He leaned back and looked at my Seminary degree on the wall. "No, I've been here before. Quite a bit, actually. No, I'm here to help with what you asked for. To help get you refocused. You just asked for it and now I'm here."

Had I been praying out loud? Had this guy been listening at the door? I turned my head in my chair. I couldn't pick out any hidden cameras.

"I don't get it," I said.

"Ask and you shall receive, Bob. You prayed for me to help so here I am to help. To give you a little guidance."

Okay, now it was getting weird.

I just stared. He stared back, the smile constant. I reached a hand over and turned the picture of Mary and James to the side so he couldn't see it.

"I'm sorry, what did you say your name was?" I thought I knew where this was going, but what else could I say?

"My name's Jesus," he said. Sure, he was still smiling, but he said it with a straight face.

"Jesus," I mumbled, my eyebrows no doubt pinching together.

"Yeah, you know." He patted my old Bible on the desk, "the guy in this book here. You've read it, right?" He laughed good at that one. Thought it was pretty funny. I didn't laugh.

"Alright, Mr. Jesus. I don't know what you're after here, but it's been a bit of a day. I'm usually up for a good joke, but maybe next week."

He got serious then. "Alright, I'm sorry Bob. Admittedly, this is not the typical way I answer prayer."

"Yeah, it's a first for me," I snarked.

"I get it," he said. "But I am who I claim to be. I do have something rather specific that I would like you to do. You asked for my help and this is how I'm going to help. In person, so to speak. You were just thinking that, in person, is so much better. To work through our issues."

I shook my head a little. I still didn't feel like I was in danger, but the guy was definitely crazy. I found a smile of my own. Let's see how he handled a little scripture thrown his way.

"Okay," I hesitated, "…Jesus. Why should I believe you? Didn't you tell us to beware of things just like this? You know, 'Watch out that no one deceives you. For many will come in my name, claiming "I am the Christ" and will deceive many'? What about that?"

His smile deepened and I saw his teeth. His eyes sparkled with genuine humor. "Well said, pastor. But listen, this is just between me and you. I'm not trying to start an uprising. This is strictly an answer to your prayer.

Your plea for help. I would think most people would be happy for such a quick response to their prayer."

"Yes, very speedy service," I agreed. "But you have to admit, it's a tough pill to swallow."

The crazy guy got serious then and set his arms on my desk and leaned towards me. I leaned back into my chair. "Seriously, Bob, I do have a mission for you, if you want to call it that. If I am really the Jesus of your Bible, would you do what I asked?"

"If you were really Jesus, then of course I would."

"Good. Because this won't be easy. It will cause stress on your life. Embarrassment, at least according to the world. This earthly world. But your Father asks it of you."

He must have saw that I was not completely sold yet. "Turn a couple pages," he said, "and read about the Samaritan woman I spoke with at Jacob's well. She didn't believe me either. Not at first. Not until I told her about her life. Then she told all that would listen and it drew more to me. More to the Father."

And then he did the same to me. Told me things that no person on this planet knew about me. And like the Samaritan woman, I was amazed and shocked and utterly in awe. I almost believed. I wanted to believe. But the Samaritan woman had been forewarned that the messiah was coming. This guy had just shown up.

"I tell you what," he said. "Remember when you first felt called to be a pastor? You were fourteen years old, and you prayed mightily then, too."

I interrupted him. "What do you mean, 'felt called'? You're saying I wasn't called?"

He waved a hand. "Bob, please. As I was saying, you were fourteen years old and had been at the summer youth camp at Lake Pleasanton. My words touched you. That's what you wanted to do. To share my word. I, myself, was very happy that day."

"That's fine, Mr. Jesus. But I've probably told that story fifty times from this pulpit. Anyone could tell you —"

It was his turn to interrupt. "Yes, many have heard that part of the story, but what about the whole story? Remember seminary? How scared you were?"

That shut me up.

He laughed. "That's right. And you felt like you'd made a mistake. That you'd misunderstood. The missions and passing out tracts and standing on street corners. Until you read Paul's letter to my church in Ephesus. You don't like to talk about that little moment of doubt. Not even with Mary."

I remained locked in my chair. He was right. I had never told anyone about that. I had doubted. Just for a bit. But when I read," *So Christ himself gave the apostles, the prophets, the evangelists, the pastors and teachers, to equip his people for works of service, so that the body of Christ may be built up,*" I was relieved. I was reassured. Even though I'd read that verse a million times, that one time was what I needed right then. To remind me that I was to help equip the saints.

I didn't do a lot of "altar calls" in my services, much to the chagrin of some of the congregation. But is that what I was to do as a pastor? I don't mean to split hairs, but the evangelist brings the sheep into the fold. I feed the sheep.

I had been scared. I was scared now. But I didn't move. Couldn't.

His hand was up again, like some Jedi mind trick gluing me to my seat. I thought of when Jesus had read the scroll in Nazareth and they were going to throw Him off a cliff, but He just walked through them as it wasn't his time. I always wondered how He did that.

"Please, Bob. I know this is hard, but I need you to listen. When the time comes, search my words and you will see their truth. But for now, just listen to what I'd have you do for my kingdom."

He straitened up. The smile receded.

"I'm going to bring you out of your calling for just a bit. Long ago I did call you to be a pastor to my flock, and you responded and I thank you for that. You have been a good servant, but you've strayed off the mark just a bit. I want to help you get back on track. But like I said, it won't be easy.

"I want you to evangelize a little for me. All you need to do is tell people the good news about their Father and how He loves them. I am going to provide you with a platform. The whole world will be able to see and hear you. In a moment of distress, the opportunity will be laid before you. You will have to choose your life or doing what I ask. I will make it plain to you, but the choice is yours."

It was a lot to take in. So many questions and ideas and feelings competed with each other that it was hard to get any coherent thought to stick together in my mind. There were doubts also, but they rapidly fell away as the man claiming to be Jesus looked at me.

I went with the first thing that came to mind: my worldly responsibilities. "What about the church? I mean the one here in Lamont. I was working on a sermon for next week."

The humor returned to his eyes. "Better than today's, hmm?"

I felt the need to explain myself. "No, this one should be good. It's a deep dive on the parable of the soils. But instead of one sermon, I was going to take four or five weeks and go over the soil types and see what we can do about cultivating our own soils. To get closer to... well, you, I guess."

Genuine confusion clouded his eyes. "The parable of the soils?" he said.

"Oh, c'mon. Where the sower throws about the seed and it falls on the different soils? It's in three of the gospels."

Recognition struck, which seemed odd for someone who was supposed to be all-knowing and all-seeing. "Ah, yes. That parable. That was a good one. I don't know if I would have called it that, but yes, a worthy parable to share.

"But, no, you are to perform your pastoral duties as well as this new item I have for you. My church still needs you here, Bob. But others do too."

"So, what do I do?" I asked.

"Follow me."

3

After he left, I stayed in my chair, silent. Just the jazz station softly playing in the background. I was sweating. And shaking. The world started to come back. Birds sang outside the window. The drip from the kitchen sink started up again. I sprang up and went out into the church parking lot, scanning around. No greasy jeans guy. No crazy curly haired guy claiming to be Jesus Christ. Nope. Only one crazy guy in this parking lot.

How could he know that?

My hand shook as I took the keys out of my pocket and slid into the driver's seat of my Ford Ranger. It was as much of a truck as I could afford, but it got the job done. I sat in there a moment as the office visit replayed in my mind. Staring up towards heaven I prayed again. Not like the on-your-knees prayer, but just my normal prayerful conversing with my creator. *Okay. What was that all about?* No immediate response this time. I peeked in the rearview: no one sneaking up behind me.

Maybe this funk of mine was real deep. Was I imagining things now? Hallucinations? I started my truck and pulled onto the main drive.

Traffic was light today. Of course, in the town of Lamont, traffic was usually light. This was a farming town on the outskirts of Bakersfield. Most towns in the San Joaquin Valley were farming communities and traffic jams typically involved slow moving tractors going from field to field.

Lamont epitomized small town. When Mary and I had moved here from Texas four years ago, that vibe drew us in. The full-time pastor position helped, as well. Sure, it got hot in the summer and the fog sometimes made travel interesting, but we'd lived in the Texas heat, so we weren't scared of anything weather related.

The small-town people had a simple faith and most of them had a tie to agriculture in some way. They had a connection to the earth and the soil and at one time I thought it perhaps gave them a small advantage of connectedness to their Creator. Now I wondered.

The park looked full as I went by. Families gathered to enjoy the weather, before it got too hot later in the year. It was well kept for this town that did not enjoy the largest budget in the state. Sure, the grass was a little sparse, but it didn't stop soccer games from being played. The spring foliage was bright green and, of course, there were blooms on a lot of the trees. It made my nose run just thinking about it.

I stopped at one of our few stop lights and looked to the buildings on the street. At one of the town's bars. I saw two cars there that had been in the church parking lot just an hour previous. Was I being a bit judgy today? Or was it the despair I felt within my congregation, within myself, that we were all just playing a game called church? And once the game was over, we went back to being whatever we wanted. *In those days Israel had no king; everyone did as they saw fit.*

Who was I to talk? I'd just been visited by Jesus and I had no idea what to do with it.

A car behind me honked. The light was green. Probably had been for a while. I politely lifted my hand in apology and started down the road again.

I pulled into the McDonald's parking lot and parked next to Dave's white Dodge. White Dodges were a dime a dozen here, but Dave's had a nice crease in the top of the tailgate to distinguish it from the rest of the herd. And the "Jesus Loves You" bumper sticker. We were close to the big city of Bakersfield, but we didn't have our own coffee shop yet. We had a Starbucks inside the Albertsons grocery store, but it was hard to have a sit down coffee there. McDonalds' coffee wasn't half bad. And it was only a buck.

I sat in the truck, gathering my thoughts. How did you explain this one? I picked up my phone and sent a text to Mary. **Crazy stuff after you left. I'll tell you tonight.**

Dave picked up two cups of coffee as I walked in and we made our way to a booth over by the restrooms, far away from the children's playground. We each scooted into the plastic benches and Dave slid one of the cups over to me.

"Thanks for the coffee, Dave. I owe you one."

"It's alright," he said. "I took a five from the offering plate." He grinned and took an investigative sip. Then another, bigger, sip, so it must not be too hot.

I took my own taste, the heat of the cup seeping into my fingers. "I need to talk to you about this morning."

He rolled his eyes. "It's okay, Bob. It really wasn't that bad."

"No. Not the sermon. The guy who came into my office afterwards. After I talked to you."

"Oh, Phil? He was the guy I was talking to after the service. I didn't think he was going to stick around."

"No, not him. A different guy. Did you see a guy with curly hair and goatee? Normal looking guy? Kind of a big nose?"

He scrunched his face and pondered the description. "No, doesn't ring any bells."

"I don't think I've ever seen him either. He comes in right after I'd got done praying and tells me that he was Jesus."

Dave raised his eyebrows. "Really? THE Jesus?"

"That's what he said."

"Well, I don't suppose he's the first guy to claim that," Dave said trying to lean back in the plastic bench but it made him sort of slump down.

I leaned forward with my hands around the warm cup. "Yeah, but this guy told me... things. Things about me. About my life. Things that other people don't know. A couple that even Mary doesn't know."

"Almost like the woman at the well."

"That's what he said," I replied.

"So, you had Jesus in your office?" A lady was walking towards the restroom. I gave Dave a can-you-keep-it-down sideways glance.

"I don't know, Dave. For a minute I was convinced."

"And now you're not?"

I slumped in my own bench. "I'm starting to think that maybe I'm just losing my marbles."

Dave looked at his Styrofoam cup and tapped a finger against its side before speaking. "You know what I saw in Africa, right?"

Dave went to Africa a lot. To a mission that Lamont Community Church supported. He had made his first trip over twenty years ago. After he and Elena had lost their baby. He had a deep love for the people over there. Especially the kids. It was really a mission to support the impoverished youth.

I think Dave would live over there fulltime if he could. On his first trip he had witnessed a miracle. He had performed it, actually. Some supernatural miracle from God. It gave Dave a certain perspective on things of that nature.

"Yes," I answered. "Your healing."

"Yeah, the healing. All I know is that sometimes God works in ways that are very different than what you or I think is normal or even right. I'm saying that if Jesus wanted to take on his human form and come visit you... well, I could believe something like that might happen."

"So, you think this guy was Jesus Christ?" He was taking this a whole lot better than I had.

"No," he said. "Most likely I think you fell asleep in your chair and dreamt the whole thing. Or you are going crazy. Either of those two scenarios seems most likely." He took another sip. That Dave, always a big help.

I gave him a scowl. "Thanks."

We both sat there saying nothing. Seemed like that's all we did mostly. He had a studious look on his face, chewing over my story in his mind.

Finally, he said, "Wait. He had a goatee? I've never seen Jesus with a goatee. And curly hair? Was it long at least?"

"No," I said quietly. I didn't know if he was making fun of me or not. Dave could go either way.

"Birkenstocks?"

"No. Some sort of tennis shoes. No robe. No halo. Just some guy."

He sighed heavy. "Bob, when that healing happened in Africa, it was totally not how I thought something like that would go down. And I've seen a lot of miraculous things that others may not classify as miracles. That guy who I talked with after church? Phil? He emptied his pockets before he left. Gave me three bucks. Said he wanted to give it to the church. Isn't that a miracle? And not by someone who looked like a miracle worker."

I looked at Dave sideways. "So, you honestly think this guy's legit?"

"Bob, I think you experienced something in there. I mean, unless you dreamt it. Is that a possibility?"

"No. At least, I don't think so. Just before he came in, though, I prayed. Prayed like I hadn't in a long time. Just reaching out to God. For help. To guide me. To help get our church off its duff. I was crying."

"Hmm," was all Dave said.

I swirled my coffee a little bit. It was almost gone. Dave stared at his own cup.

"You said he asked you to do something. What was it?"

"He said he wanted me to preach the word. Not like I have been, but in some big way. He said he'd provide the opportunity and then I could do what he said or not. Said it might kill me or something like that. Like it was going to be a big deal."

Dave drained the last of his coffee. "Well, then, it will be easy. Either it will happen or not. Then you'll know, won't you."

"You're not being as helpful as I thought you were going to be."

He laughed and said, "Sorry, Bob, Elvis sightings, maybe. But Jesus sightings are uncharted territory for me."

He took on a serious tone. "Look, I know you are going through something and something did happen to you. I wish I could explain it, but I'm with you. You know that."

"Yeah," I said, but not as cheery as I wanted. What did I expect? That Dave was going to say Oh yeah, I saw that guy, he's definitely the Savior.

My pocket buzzed. A text from Mary.

I maneuvered off the bench. "Thanks for the coffee. I'm headed home. Mary's back but she wants me to get some milk on the way."

Dave got up, too. "Sounds a little mundane for someone who got to talk with Jesus today."

I finally loosened up and laughed too. "Yeah, my big mission from God. 'Don't forget the milk.'"

4

Lamont had a big grocery store but it was across town so I pulled into the liquor store on the corner of Main and Road 43. They carried milk and I didn't feel like dealing with the Sunday grocery crowd. A man named Marcos Valentine owned the liquor store and often worked the Sunday shift. He and I had a small sort of relationship. I came in at least once a week and got a candy bar or soda or something like that and I would push a little Jesus Marcos's way. He was good natured about it and asked a lot of questions, which was good. He was genuinely curious, so I kept trying to plant the seed.

Marcos saw me come in and gave a small wave as he rang up a customer's pile of decidedly unhealthy food choices. I nodded in return and went to the back of the store where the refrigerated items were. I had to make my way past a couple of teens in the candy aisle. I pulled a half gallon of 2% out and checked the expiration date. Marcos was a nice guy, but I didn't know if milk was a big mover at a liquor store. Still a week left. Good to go.

Closing the glass panel, I looked up into one of those concave mirrors that sometimes hung in the ceilings of certain stores and noticed a young Hispanic guy fidgeting in the corner. Not like a lot of the young men in Lamont where the attire was typically jeans or shorts and t-shirts. No, this kid had baggy pants and a bulky hoodie sweatshirt. A large silver chain went from one of his belt loops into his pocket. Quite frankly, he looked like one of the gang members you might see in some of the not so nice neighborhoods in Bakersfield. In the mirror I couldn't see if he had any tattoos or not.

    I chastised myself a bit. It wasn't very fair of me, much less all that Christian, to be judging this poor kid based on his image in the mirror. I thought about the familiar vehicles in the bar's parking lot again. How did I know what sort of person he was? Maybe I should go say hi. If he really was a stranger here, I should welcome him. Although I doubted I was very good company today.

    He walked out of my view in the mirror. The teenagers in the candy aisle started giggling about something and I looked over and saw one of the girls showing the other something on her phone. I started to make a judgement on them too, but held myself back. Probably the Spirit held me back, because I was indeed in a judgy mood.

    The young kid was at the counter and I came up behind him with my milk in one hand and pulled out my wallet with the other. When I looked back up, I saw Marcos' face over the kid's shoulder and my first reaction was that the store owner was having some sort of medical issue. His face was contorted and the color drained away.

    Then I saw the gun in the kid's hand.

    I dropped the milk and the plastic bounced hard on the linoleum floor, ricocheting into the kid's calf. He whipped around, sticking the gun right in my face.

    I raised my hands in the air like I'd seen so many times on TV. The barrel of the gun was inches from my face. I smelled something. Gunpowder, I think. That cordite aroma I remembered from going to the gun range when I was a kid.

    My heart started pounding and I felt a little nauseous. My senses focused to laser precision, though. I could smell the day-old food beneath the heat lamps by the register. My ears picked up a choked off screech from one of the girls in the candy aisle. I thought I heard Marcos take a huge gulp. Or maybe that was me. My mouth was very dry all of a sudden.

My eyes started to pick up all sorts of details. Past the gun I could see the kids face. How scared and nervous he looked. The beads of sweat on his forehead. He looked even younger than I had thought in the mirror. Beyond him I could see Marcos, his face still pale and scared and confused. Like he didn't know what to do.

He had his hands up, too.

And I could pick up every detail of the gun in the kid's hand. The blued steel and the fake wooden grip poking out just below his palm, his knuckles white, his index finger on the trigger. The gun was a revolver and I could see into the holes of the cylinder and saw the jacketed slugs of pistol rounds waiting to be unleashed.

And that huge black void full of unknown violent potential just inches from my face.

"Hold on, buddy. Let's settle down." Was I talking to the kid or trying to reassure myself?

"Shut up, man!" the kid yelled at me, his face taking on the look of a cornered rabbit. Maybe my first inclination, or judgement if you like, was correct. Maybe he was a gang member from Bakersfield. Clint Jones was a cop that went to our church and he dealt with gang members. Hadn't he told me that part of the Bako-M gangs' initiation was to rob a place? A way to prove yourself. To prove that you had what it took. That you belonged.

Robbery was a good initiation. Shooting a cop was another. Shooting a pastor was probably almost as good.

This time I knew it was me that gulped.

The gun shook even more and the kid looked more nervous than ever. "Back away. Just back up!" he yelled, his voice cracking. I tried to step back but bumped into a chips stand.

What had the Jesus-guy said to me? *In a moment of distress, the opportunity will be laid before you.*

I noticed the security camera behind Marcos and the register, pointing right at me.

A bag of chips hit the floor.

I glanced over my shoulder to see both of the girls cowering in the candy aisle, but their cell phones pointed my way, recording the whole thing. Maybe live-streaming for all I knew. I heard *the whole world will be able to see you* in my head as I thought about this entire scene going viral.

The kid's eyes were wide now as he stretched his hand with the gun even closer to my face.

You will have to choose your life or doing what I ask.

Oh no. I thought about Mary and my heart yearned for her. I regretted all the times I could have told her that I loved her but didn't. How would Dave take this? And Elena? What about Matthew? Would he even take his earbuds out when he heard?

And James? He was still so young. Didn't he need a father? To guide him in this world?

Desperate, I prayed in my head and asked God to tell me what to do and the words of the Jesus-guy came back at me again:

Tell people the good news about their Father and how He loves them.

The choice is yours.

Follow me.

The kid shook the gun. "Get away, man! I'll shoot you!"

I swallowed hard and looked right into that kid's eyes. Brown eyes full of fear and angst and downtrodden by the world in which he lived. "I don't think you will. Or maybe you will. I don't know. But I met Jesus today.

Really met Him. And He told me some things and I thought maybe they were for me, but now I think maybe they were for you."

His eyes clouded with disbelief as his head tilted sideways. I took a deep breath and evangelized. "Listen to me. I don't know you or your situation. But I have a message just for you. Your Father, your Father in Heaven loves you. You and I are sinners but we have a God that loves us to no end. A love we cannot even fathom. And He wants us in His kingdom and the only way to get there is to believe in His Son Jesus.

"Put down the gun. You know this isn't right. You know this isn't what God wants for you. Let me tell you about Jesus. About my savior. About your savior."

For just a second, just the briefest of moments, I thought the kid was going to set the gun down. Or at least lower it. But his eyes changed. They filled with hate. Like the whole world hated me. And I saw his finger tighten on the trigger.

CLICK!

I squeezed my eyes shut at the sound and involuntarily jumped a little. When I opened them, the kid was staring wild-eyed at the gun in his hand.

He looked back at me and whispered, "You're crazy, man."

The cylinder started to rotate around. A jacketed bullet fell in front of the raising hammer and then ... CLICK!

CLICK! CLICK! CLICK! CLICK!

Now the kid looked terrified of me. His head jerked back and forth. Looking for an answer. A way out. He dropped the pistol like it was on fire and ran out the door, one hand trying to keep his baggy pants up.

I looked at Marcos whose mouth was wide open in disbelief. He still had his hands in the air. I realized I still had mine up too.

***

The liquor store filled up with sheriff's officers and a couple of detectives from Bakersfield who were there to look into the possible gang angle. They asked me, Marcos, and the two girls from the candy aisle endless questions as their cruisers sat outside announcing to the world that something had gone down at the liquor store. Several times I heard the word "crazy" come from one of the girls. She would glance my way when she said it.

The detectives had me relive the ordeal in detail and I tried to leave nothing out. They went over the surveillance footage with a laptop right there onsite before making a copy to take back to their lab or office or whatever they had in the city. They also obtained copies of the girl's cell phone footage and asked them not to post any of it online yet. But it turned out that ship had already sailed, the teenage girls having immediately uploaded it to their various social media accounts.

Detective Verez interviewed me the most. After about the thirtieth time going over the events of the afternoon, he put his notepad away and I thought maybe we were done. I took a drink from the bottled water someone had given me.

He started to get out of the chair he was sitting in, but stopped and sat back down. "So, you're a preacher, eh?" he asked, but of course he knew this because we'd gone over all of this and he was a detective, so I figured he was a stickler for detail.

"Yeah," I said.

"And you told him about Jesus?" He had his head cocked, his brow scrunched together in confusion. Just like the kid had.

"Yeah," I repeated.

He leaned back and crossed his arms. "Because Jesus told you to?"

"Yeah," I said a third time and left it at that. We'd been over all of that many times, too. My whole day. I left out the part about how bad the sermon was because it didn't seem relevant and it had already taken a lot of time explaining my encounter with a guy who claimed to be Jesus. I wanted to say something about how Jesus told all of His believers to tell others about Him, but I decided the detective probably wasn't interested in theology at the moment and I had a bad track record with delivering divine messages today, so I let it go.

He stood up and moved his hands to his pants pockets. "I tell you what, Pastor, I've never heard of anything like this. Your part at least. I deal with hold ups all the time, but your response is a first. I wouldn't recommend trying it again."

"Yeah," I said one more time. It seemed the only word I was capable of uttering anymore.

He walked away, and I was unsupervised for the first time in the last couple of hours. I found one of the original sheriffs who'd been first on the scene and walked over to him. He was typing something into a tablet with a Kern County logo on it.

He looked up as I approached. "Hey, Pastor. How are you doing?"

"Good, I think. Am I about done here?"

"Yes. I know it's a lot, but that was one of the Bako-M gang members here today. The detectives got some video footage from a place across the street that got a plate off of his car. A car known in town as affiliated with Bako-M. You were lucky. They can be a rough group."

I wanted to say "yeah" again, but fought the urge. "Pretty lucky," was all I could come up with.

The Sheriff leaned in close to my ear. I could smell the peppermint of his gum. "I didn't get too good of a look at that gun. They're going to try and get prints off of it, but those sure looked like live shells. Maybe the hammer wasn't hitting the primers or something, but I saw those girls cell phone clips and I could hear the clicks."

He shook his head side to side and let out a soft whistle. "Man. Like a miracle or something."

He looked me in the eye again. "And you talked with some guy who said he was Jesus today?"

"Yeah," I said before I could stop myself.

He whistled softly again and grinned. "Man, I'm gonna have to start going to your church."

I shook Marcos' hand before I left and told him if I could do anything else to let me know. He apologized profusely, like because he owned the place it was his fault. When I pushed through the glass door and headed to my Ranger it was dark and the red and blue lights from the Sheriff's patrol cars were still strobing around and around. There was one news van there with a reporter from Channel 6 that I recognized. That seemed kind of odd to me. Sure, this was big news in Lamont, but it didn't seem like the sort of thing that would drag down a reporter from a big news program. Channel 6 was out of Fresno.

Whatever. I'd had enough mysteries for one day. I walked to my truck unnoticed. I didn't know at the time that it would be a while before I got to go anywhere unnoticed.

I sat behind the wheel and saw my cellphone laying in the passenger seat. I grabbed it up and touched the screen to see if Mary had called. She had. And so had another hundred people or so. Missed calls and texts crowded my phone. I thought about calling Mary but this wasn't something you could really explain over the phone. Not when you'd be home in ten minutes.

Closing my eyes, I set my hands on the steering wheel and pushed back in the seat. My head leaned against the rear window. Had that really happened? Was it over? I started to melt into the seat as my muscles tried to loosen up.

THORNS

My phone buzzed next to me and I opened an eye.

I just couldn't handle the thought of all those other calls. I would have to deal with them, but later. Word sure did travel fast in this little town.

I started the Ranger and drove home.

And, yes, I did forget the milk.

5

When I walked through the door, Mary rushed into my arms. She hugged me tight, resting her head on my shoulder. I hugged her back and it seemed a strange reception, but not all bad either. It's nice to be wanted.

"I forgot the milk," I said.

Her sobs turned into laughter as she pulled back from our embrace but kept one of my hands in hers as we walked into the kitchen. I sat at our small dining table and Mary went to the stove. She turned on a burner and I closed my eyes, letting the craziness of the day ebb away.

I heard her crack an egg shell and opened my eyes. "Breakfast for dinner?" I asked.

"Yes," she said. "I didn't get much done this afternoon. Too much worrying about you."

"Man, news sure travels fast around here. You should see all of the messages I have on my phone."

She turned from the eggs and looked at me, one hand on her hip, holding a spatula. Her head cocked to the side and her face seemed to insinuate that I was mentally slow. It almost made me laugh. A mock look of anger sat on her face. It was so out of place on Mary that it just struck me as humorous. Fortunately, though, I had the good sense not to laugh.

"Bob, you are all Lamont — and everywhere else — is talking about. You are all over the news and the internet and there's videos of you in that store." Her head lowered and her voice softened, "And that man had a gun right in your face." She turned back to the eggs.

I got up, went over, and wrapped my arms around her from behind. Her hair smelled clean and beautiful. She was sobbing, but I put my chin on her shoulder and she rested her head against the side of my face. "I'm sorry," I said.

I took in the scene of our quiet little kitchen and how it contrasted to the crazy world I had just left. The walls of the kitchen were a light yellow. There were some pictures hung in there, along with a couple of cute little bible quotes and a cross. A picture of me and Mary and James at the beach on a trip to the coast a couple of years ago served as the centerpiece.

She broke my embrace and I stood back so she could flip the eggs.

***

The clink of silverware against porcelain serenaded our evening dinner. I mopped up the last of my egg with a piece of toast and washed it down with the last swallow of water in my glass. Milk would have really hit the spot. I grabbed my plate, and Mary's too, and took them to the sink. Mary came in behind me and opened the dishwasher, taking the plates from me and loading them.

"I'm worried about you, Bob."

"What, cholesterol?" I asked. "I believe the latest studies now say eggs are good for you."

It's nice that I can still make Mary laugh. I love her laugh.

"No, smart guy. This mood you've been in lately. And then this robbery thing this afternoon."

"Yeah. And my sermon was horrible." She laughed again, but I wasn't trying to be funny that time.

She grabbed my hand and looked into my face. "Bob, did you really see Jesus today? That's what they're saying on the news. That you met Jesus and he told you to talk to this guy."

A truck drove by outside. Loud. Probably an exhaust issue.

I'd gone over it a thousand times today, but I went through my day again. The meeting with Jesus, the mission, the liquor store. Forgetting the milk.

"Bob," she said, hesitantly, "Uhm, Jesus coming to meet you seems a little... weird."

"I know," I said. "He just showed up. Told me what He wanted me to do."

"But how do you know it was Him? Not some crazy guy off the street? We get those, you know."

I raised my hands. "Yeah, I know. And that's what I thought. I talked with Dave about it. I argued with myself about it. At first, of course I thought it was some crazy guy. I mean, He didn't have the white robes or an entourage of angels behind Him. Not even a halo. But He knew me."

She didn't look convinced and looked at me with sympathy, like I was a sick child. Like I would get better and then we could all move past this.

"He told me something else," I said. "Something that He said would drive home the point that He was who He said He was."

She looked expectantly at me now. Curious, but still a little concerned for my mental well-being.

"He told me about the difference between pastoring and evangelizing, and I know that sounds like not a big thing, but it was a big thing to me once. It had a huge effect on how I pastor. That I even became a pastor. It wasn't something totally earth shattering, except to me."

I raised my eyebrows and looked at her, willing for her to see, but I couldn't tell for sure how she was feeling.

"Does that make sense?"

Silence. I heard her swallow. "Bob, it makes sense to you. But it makes me more worried for you. About you. That this is a remnant of your slump here lately. I mean, seeing Jesus? How does that look?"

That was maybe the worse part of the entire ordeal. That Mary didn't believe me. That she thought I'd gone crazy. Mary had always supported me, always had my back. And I, hers. But she didn't believe me.

***

I peeked in James' door before heading to bed. It wasn't often that I didn't get to see him before he went down, but the few occasions it happened, I couldn't help feeling a little bit bad. But it was time for me to hit the sack as well. I was beat. Mary had to get up early tomorrow to go to the hospital where she worked as a nurse. It wasn't a competition, but I think she probably helped more people than I did.

I had my lamp going on my nightstand and was trying to read. Christian fiction. I didn't do a lot of recreational reading, but tried to, at least on Sundays. To try and relax. But I couldn't focus on the story or the characters tonight without my brain going back to the events of the day. Sometimes Christian fiction wasn't all that compelling anyway. And sometimes it wasn't all that Christian.

Mary came out of the bathroom and got under the covers. I set the open book down on my chest and she gave me a goodnight kiss.

"G'night, Bob," she said.
"G'night, babe."

I left the light on, and she rolled the other way. My eyelids sagged, but I wanted to talk to her more about ... well, I didn't know what. We had covered all the bases, but I still felt like I needed to work through it. I guess I had experienced something incredibly supernatural and I couldn't just stew on it. I needed to flap my gums about it. Must be the pastor in me.

But if I wanted to talk to Mary tonight, I had better get with it. That woman could sleep anywhere, anytime, and it wouldn't take her long to nod off.

"So, how did youth group go today?" It was all I could come up with.

Mary helped with the youth program at the church. We had a young guy that led the group, but Mary helped out with the older high school aged kids. Kids like Matthew who probably didn't take his earbuds out the whole time. Besides, she was already a nurse, so to complete the pastor's wife stereotype she had to volunteer with the youth as well.

She rolled on her back and my lamp cast shadows on her skin. "It was fine. Nothing out of the normal. No Jesus sightings."

She nudged my leg with her foot under the covers at her attempt at humor.

"Very funny," I said.

She turned her head to look at me, joke time over. "We did talk about this concert coming up next weekend in Bakersfield, though. Some horrible band that a lot of these kids listen to. Tried to persuade them not to go. Or show them the silliness of it. Or the lack of anything Godly in the music. I don't know if it got through to any of them or if it just made them want to go more."

I folded my novel and set the book on the stand and turned out the light. I took her hand in mine and said, "Hey, you guys are doing a good work with those kids. You know that. But they are young minds in this world. We can only do so much. Especially with those older ones. We can only advise and hope they don't have to learn too many hard lessons on their own."

Her teeth glinted in the moonlight coming through our window. "I know. Sometimes you see what they're interested in, though, and wonder if what you're doing is what you're supposed to be doing."

I hoped I gave her a little comfort with my comments. It also wasn't lost on me that the thoughts going through her head mirrored my own exasperation from earlier. Maybe the whole reason for my off mood lately. It was sometimes disheartening to do what you thought you were supposed to be doing, what you felt God had called you to do, and get what felt like no response from those around you. Like you were invisible.

It was the same train of thought that had led to the prayer in my office and my encounter with the Jesus guy. I didn't know why I kept thinking of Him as the Jesus guy. He was Jesus, right? He'd told me all these things. And I'd had this encounter today and it played out how He said. I'd had to look at a gun and thought I was going to die and pick Him or me. And I'd followed Him. Without hesitation. Was it wrong to feel a little pride in that?

Maybe that's what I really wanted to talk about with Mary. For her to tell me that it was how I thought it was and that I'd done well. I wanted her to believe me. I wanted her to be excited. But I didn't want to bring that back up. Not yet.

"A pretty bad band, huh?"

"Yeah," she said through a half yawn. "Bad band. They're called Lucifer. I mean, how blatantly bad could you be? You should hear the words to their songs. Well, the parts where you can actually understand what they're saying."

I grunted. Our kids? From our church? Going to watch something like that?

"Maybe I should call their parents tomorrow. Do they know what's going on?"

"Yes, we've told them. None of the kids will admit they're going, but they put all of this stuff on the internet and forget their Sunday friends can see what's there. We know some of them are going."

"Matthew Liston?" I asked.

"For sure Matthew's going," she said, no doubt in her voice.

It wasn't just a testament to the kids and their behavior or ideals. It was the grown ups that had to look after and teach and disciple these kids. How could their parents allow this? How could their parents' pastor allow this? It seemed to reaffirm every thought I'd had earlier today. That my people were not getting the message somehow. Or they had a poor messenger. Ouch.

Mary pulled her hand from mine and stretched her arms before rolling back over again. Then out of the blue, with sleep heavy in her speech she said, "They don't even call it a stage that they perform on. They call it the 'alter' or the 'platform' or something like that."

I looked through the darkness at our ceiling. A platform?

I am going to provide a platform. The whole world will be able to see and hear you.

I was sure that was just how He put it earlier in my office. A platform. And this crazy thought came into my head, like I was supposed to go to this concert and ... what? Preach? Evangelize? He'd said that, too. Maybe I was supposed to go and just share with whoever I could at this thing. Be the light in the middle of this darkness. Maybe it would be just as life threatening as the gun had been.

I was going to ask Mary what she thought, but she was lightly snoring already. The woman had a gift, I swear.

So, instead, I snuck out of bed and went into the dark living room and, for the second time that day, got down on my knees and prayed. I tried to be heartfelt and recreate the feeling of earlier, but it somehow fell flat. I asked for guidance and wisdom and to do what He'd have me do. I sat and tried to calm my thoughts and let Him speak to me.

I heard a car go by on the road outside. No muffler issues. It didn't stop. Finally, I got off my knees and sat on the couch in the dark. The little red light on the TV blinked at me. Like it wondered what I was doing. No one knocked on the door. No great epiphanies from above. I thought I heard crickets outside.

It started to get cold, just sitting on my couch in the dark in my underwear, so I finally went back to bed. Eventually I fell asleep.

6

I was up early with Mary as she got ready for her shift at the hospital. She bustled about packing a lunch and I watched in silence, sipping coffee. We hadn't said much. It was still kind of awkward. Maybe she thought I'd forgotten about it. Or she hoped I had. Or she hoped she'd dreamt it. But I had the TV on with Closed Captioning going so I could keep an eye on the news from the kitchen.

She stopped on her way past the TV as a story about last night popped up. There I was, talking with the kid with the gun. It hadn't been a dream. I could read my own words about Jesus telling me that I was supposed to talk with the kid.

Mary turned from the TV and looked at me, trying to create a smile. "I can't believe that happened last night."

I knew she was avoiding the meeting with Jesus. It was uncomfortable because I had said this thing, and she didn't believe it. It was not comfortable for me either. It pained me to not be on the same page as my wife.

But a night's rest had not tempered an excitement I felt also. Jesus had come to my office and spoke directly to me. Given me a mission. Now I just had to work out how to handle it.

"Yeah, almost as crazy as Jesus coming to see me."

Uncomfortable or not, I needed to discuss it.

Setting her lunch and purse on the counter, she sat on a stool and her shoulders slumped forward as she stared at me.

"Bob, I know something happened yesterday and you think you saw something, but Jesus? In the flesh? It's just so out there."

"I know. But it happened. I just wish I could get you to believe me."

She took my hands, and while I didn't see belief in her eyes, I did see love. That helped.

"Baby, I want to believe you, but... I don't know. I don't want to lie to you. At the hospital, we see people who go through traumatic ordeals and sometimes their brains create things to help them cope. It's just –"

"Look, it happened, Mary," I said, my voice rising a tick. She glanced towards the hallway. I lowered my voice so as to not wake up James.

"Look, whatever it is, I have to keep going forward with it. I don't think the liquor store was the only thing He wanted me to do. There's more coming, I'm sure of it."

I looked at the ceiling, not knowing what else to say. I groped for the words to help her at least see where I was coming from. To convince her I wasn't losing my marbles.

She looked down at me and tilted her head. "Bob, you know that I love you and always support you. I'll try to understand. I'll talk to Dr. Stanley about it."

Which wasn't exactly what I wanted to hear. Dr. Stanley was a psychiatrist that made rounds in the hospital once a week. Yep, she thought I was crazy.

She grabbed her stuff and leaned over to give me a kiss on the cheek.

"I've got to go. Call me if you need anything. I know God still has plans for you. If you really wanted to do something, you should do something about that concert."

THORNS

The door closed and I sat in silence. I heard the muffled sounds of her car starting.

Oh, I planned on doing something about the concert.

***

I usually didn't go down to the church on Mondays until later in the afternoon. Mondays were a day off. Most people were of the mindset that pastors only worked once a week, but that was hardly the case. The time to build a sermon every week, especially when you were having a hard time seeing even a semblance of where God was leading you, was extensive. Or maybe I was just slow. But it took me a lot of time.

The rest of the week I tried to be consistent with my time at the church. I kept regular office hours and there was always some task or repair that needed to be handled. I didn't want to become complacent or take for granted what Lamont Community Church was able to provide me. It wasn't every pastor that was able to lead a congregation that afforded him a livable wage. Where my only job was pastoring this church. It really was a blessing and maybe that's why I was so down on what I perceived as a lack of response from those under my stead.

Maybe it was my pride that was hurt. I realized that was a distinct possibility. I didn't like to think of it that way, but I was human and therefore very much concerned about me. I would like to be the servant that Christ modeled for me, but often my ego liked to cut in line.

But on this Monday, I dropped James off at school, drove down to the church, went into my office, and turned my phone back on. I'd shut it down last night when the notifications and texts and messages wouldn't stop. The landline for the church phone even had three messages on it. I don't think I'd had three messages on it the last five years. Landlines: how antiquated.

The main goal of the day, however, had to do with the phone. Most of these calls were from people in the congregation concerned for my welfare and I owed them a response. As I went through my voicemails, the tone I detected seemed not so much a concern for my welfare, but digging for something to feed the gossip chain. Churches were good for that, too.

I wrote down all of the calls that I needed to return and then went to the texts. Forty-six. I decided not to dive into those just yet. My computer had finally warmed up so I looked at the emails. Oh boy, now the task seemed overwhelming. The best course of action seemed also the most cowardly: a mass email to the congregation.

I constructed the text of the email and read it over several times, tweaking a word here and there. I thanked everyone for their concern, yes, I was okay, blah, blah, blah. There wasn't a whole slew of details that I could share regarding what had happened at the liquor store. The police told me to try to be selective in what I'd shared as they investigated the crime. That was fine by me.

I left out the part about meeting Jesus. It was a touchy part of the story. I mean, yes, it had happened, but I could see the eye rolls and doubts and I didn't want to deal with it. I would have to, but I wanted to put more thought into that particular email. Not that I could blame the doubters. It was a crazy story. Even now I found doubt about the whole thing tugging at the edge of my perception.

Of course I called Dave. He was riled up. He told me it was proof that I hadn't been dreaming. He wanted to meet up for lunch but I made an excuse of wanting to decompress over things by myself and said we'd get together later this week.

THORNS

I hit the play button on the answering machine. One call was from Elmira Sanchez, an older lady who regularly attended Sunday service and who thought cell phones were instruments of the devil so wouldn't use one. Evidently, she wouldn't call one either.

The second call was from the Bakersfield Californian, the newspaper over in the big city looking for a comment or maybe an interview. And then the third message was from the NBC affiliate out of Fresno asking for the same thing.

I leaned back in my chair. A failed holdup attempt was not really news worthy. Not in Fresno or Bakersfield. No, this had to do with the part about talking with Jesus. Why had I brought that up? Not that I was ashamed of it or of Him, but it wasn't a good look. It would offer an opportunity for them to mock our church. Our faith.

Matthew came to mind. Not Matthew who ignored the world via pieces of plastic jammed in his ears, but Matthew, the tax collector: *Blessed are you when people insult you, persecute and falsely say all kinds of evil against you because of me.* Then the words Jesus spoke to me in my office on Sunday: *Because this won't be easy. It will cause stress on your life. Embarrassment, at least according to the world.*

The troubling thing was that the embarrassment part caused me more anxiety than the persecution part. That ego again.

What if the media was part of what He was asking me to do? What better platform than that? Or worst, depending on how you looked at it. Small sound bites telling whatever story some editor thought should be put out there. Maybe it wasn't the concert, but the news media?

I did feel a little stressed out. Prophecy fulfilled on that account.

The idea of platform again reared its head so I decided to look into this band that was playing on Saturday. I Googled "Lucifer band" and the group's website popped up. I clicked the link thinking I better clear my browser history after this one. An image of a pentagram appeared on my screen and fire and guys in black leather and chains were on a stage (platform, I guess) jumping around, ripping on their electric guitars, their heads bouncing up and down.

The biggest surprise was my speakers. As soon as the image came up, the group's music started blasting through my computer's speakers. I don't know what I had last listened to over the computer, but I had the volume all the way up. I almost fell out of my chair. I stood and tried to clear a path through the books and papers on my desk to find the volume control for the speakers.

Somehow in all of that noise I picked out something that didn't belong. A different rhythm that my brain finally processed as a knocking on my office door. I glanced back from my volume control search to see the door handle turn and the door itself start to open inward.

Great. This ought to be fun.

***

Dave hurried into the office with a look of concern. I finally found the volume knob and turned the assaulting noise off. Plopping back into my chair, I gave him a smile. You know, just another day at the office. Nothing weird about walking in on your pastor blasting death metal with a pentagram on his desktop.

"Hey, Dave."

"Uhm, hi pastor." He looked around my office, the concern on his face replaced by confusion.

Satisfied no sacrifices lay in hiding, he turned back to me. "Are you okay?"

"Yeah. It's a bit of a story."

I forgot that Dave came by on Mondays after lunch. I hadn't realized how the day had been slipping by. He came to clean up the sanctuary and make sure the kitchen was ready for Sunday. He also set up the small conference room for an AA group that met here on Monday evenings. You know, the little things that have to get done at a church by someone. Someone who usually gets no recognition or accolades but faithfully serves in that regard anyway.

"You still need to decompress?" he asked.

"Naw," I said, indicating one of the chairs. "Have a seat if you've got a minute."

He sat down. "Sure. Are we going to discuss your new musical preferences?"

"No," I chuckled. "I'd kind of like to talk about yesterday. I hope you've got your elder cap on, because I could use some guidance."

"I don't know, Bob. I doubt I can do much better than the guy you met with yesterday."

"Yeah, well, He wasn't incredibly specific."

He looked at me solemnly. Dave could joke around with the best of them, but he was incredibly spiritual, and could be serious when appropriate.

"I heard your little crime stopping escapade has made quite an impact. Viral videos, reposts, all that good stuff. Such a funny way for the Lord to do things. Which I suppose shouldn't surprise us. What do you need help with?"

I took on a serious tone, too. "I don't think it's done, Dave. I think He's got more to do with me."

"Well, of course He does."

"No, I mean more things like what happened last night. I don't think that's the culmination of it."

"Did He come see you again?"

"No, but... I just think there's more."

He looked at me and we sat in silence, reminiscent of our talk in McDonalds. I could barely hear the drip from the kitchen sink.

I turned back to my computer and rotated it around so he could see the screen. "See these guys, here?"

"Yeah. That the new worship team?"

I gave him a look to remind him to stay in serious mode. He held up his hands.

"No. But this band is playing in Bakersfield this Saturday. I think I'm going to go there. Some of our youth kids want to go to this thing."

"What are you going to do there, Bob?"

What was I going to do there? I didn't know. But I wasn't going to let that slow me down. "I'll do whatever the Lord leads me to do." I said it smugly. How could anyone refute such powerful arguments?

Unfortunately, Dave was not fazed by my use of Christianese. "Bob, if some missionary came to ask you for money, you'd ask him what his plan was. If they said what you just told me, you would laugh in their face." How could I reject that pearl of truth?

I tried again. "I think that Jesus wants me to go to that concert this weekend. To teach the gospel to anyone who will listen to it. Does that sound crazy?"

"Yes!"

"Dave, when I saw Jesus, he said that He would provide the platform. He used that exact word: platform. You know what they call the stage that these guys perform on?"

"Platform. Yeah, I know." He looked defeated.

"Does it still sound crazy?"

Dave's attitude shifted. "You know what, Bob? After yesterday, how crazy could it be? But I think it is sold out so good luck getting in."

I clicked on a couple of tabs on the group's website and there was the date and the venue on their schedule page. Sure enough, the concert was sold out. Which was sort of a relief because I didn't really want to go there, but it was also disheartening. My Sunday services didn't sell out, but this stuff?

I slouched in my chair. "Maybe the liquor store was all that Jesus wanted me to say. The video went viral. It was on the news. I suppose the word got out that way. It was just that last night, I thought he wasn't done with me. In this regard, I mean. Whatever this particular mission is."

"Well, pastor, I imagine if he wants you to be at that concert, he'll open the door for you." This from the guy who ten seconds ago was trying to talk me out of it. But it was also a very Dave thing to say. With no clear direction, you left it in God's hands. Probably where we should always start.

"I suppose so," I said. "How do these kids even get this stuff? How don't their parents know?"

He gave me a sideways look that made me feel much older than I was. "Pastor, they play Lucifer on the radio. 106.1, I think."

I don't know how Dave knew that.

He must have recognized the question lurking behind my lips, but he hopped out of the chair. "Well, I've got a couple more things to get ready in the conference room." He gave a me grin before walking out the door. "I'm glad you're okay pastor. Try to keep it down in here though."

***

On the way home I stopped at the grocery store, not the corner liquor store. I did remember the milk this time and I picked up a couple more items for the week and for dinner that night. I received a couple looks at the store, but maybe I was just being paranoid.

I turned on the radio when I left and scrolled the dial to 106.1 to see what these kids were listening to and what passed for music these days. It made me feel a little like a grumpy old man, but maybe that was the direction I was headed anyway.

Some loud and fast beat with a lot of drums and electric guitar was coming to an end once I got the dial settled on the station. Then the DJ came on with his used car salesman's voice.

"Hey everybody, are we ready for the Lucifer concert on Saturday? Do you have your tickets? If you don't, well, guess what? You're out of luck."

The DJ laughed and they played some game show sound effect that would normally play when someone got the big question wrong. I scowled at the radio like it was mocking me.

The DJ came back on again. "Well, maybe you're not totally out of luck. We here at Hard Rock 106.1 don't want you to feel left out just because you waited till the last minute. We've got one ticket left and we're giving it away right now. You just have to be caller one-oh-six and you could be seeing Lucifer Saturday at Mechanics Bank Arena! Last chance!"

The DJ gave out the number to call and went into another song. *I'm sure he'll open a door for you,* Dave had said. I turned the radio back off and looked at my cell phone. Well, I wasn't going to talk on my phone and drive. Not this time, at least.

I pulled into our driveway and reached to grab the grocery bags. I spotted my phone sitting on the seat, daring me. I looked towards the heavens. Really?

I picked up the cell phone and dialed the number from memory. Which would probably work in my favor, since my memory wasn't all that great most of the time. I would probably just get a busy signal. Who knows how many people were calling the number right now.

I had been all over this idea just a little bit ago, but now? Well, it didn't seem to make as much sense. Dave was right. It was crazy. I had no plan. I had no clue what I was getting into. A slight breeze wafted through the truck and rattled the plastic bags holding the groceries. The sweet smell of tree blossoms infiltrated my senses. I thought about hanging up. If I got a busy signal I was dropping this crazy idea.

But I didn't get a busy signal. My call was picked up by a familiar sounding voice. One I had just been listening to on the radio. "Congratulations," it said. "You're one lucky dog. You're caller one-oh-six and you're going to see Lucifer on Saturday night!"

Crap.

7

Mechanics Bank Arena was a huge venue in Bakersfield that housed sporting events and concerts. The brightly lit sign exclaiming its location was visible for miles out and I drove my little Ranger a little slower than what I normally would. Mary had reiterated her displeasure with this idea. I was liking it less and less. James had wanted to go with me. Not that he knew about the band, thank God, but he just thought going to a concert with his dad would be fun.

But even Mary couldn't help but see God's hand in this. Not the way it played out getting the ticket. It was like sending a missionary into a Muslim country. Well, that's what Dave said, but I thought he was overplaying the danger angle a little bit.

He was serious when he lightly grabbed my arm. "No, Bob, but it could be dangerous. I cannot imagine people who listen to music like that really want to hear what you have to say."

"Maybe they are the ones who need to hear it more than anyone else," I'd said and it sounded way more confident than I felt. My pat Christian response worked on Dave's defenses this time.

I pulled into the parking lot and it was jam-packed with cars already. The Lucifer crowd acted like this was a tailgate party before the big game. There were BBQs going and a lot of red plastic cups that I imagined contained more than lemonade.

And the sound. The noise that emanated from portable speakers and from vehicle sound systems was just that: noise. I didn't see how it could be called music. But this was what the youth of my church was listening to. And from what few words I could understand, Mary and the rest of the youth leadership were right to warn the kids off of this stuff.

I needed to focus. I needed to lose the grumpy old man mentality. I asked God to soften my heart towards the people here. Besides, when James went to college, this would be "classic rock."

I found a parking spot far away from the entrance and looked at my watch. Funny, my hand seemed to be trembling. The concert started in half an hour but the gates were open and people filed that direction. I said another prayer right there next to my truck that God would lead me. And that He hopefully wasn't just having a good laugh on my account.

Apparently, I should have thought about my wardrobe a bit. Dark colors were everywhere. Shirts, sweaters, jeans, hats. All black, the only color coming from chains and logos on clothing. Logos that depicted images of evil and violence and foul language. I hadn't worn my white hat, but the coloring of my shirt and pants, just light blue and khaki mind you, stood out like a mirage in the desert.

Smoke hung in the air as well. Smelled like a skunk factory. The event was a rebellion of sorts. Against the status quo and what society deemed was appropriate. But it was also a rebellion against the things that God stood for. Holy things. Besides, how rebellious were you when everyone else was doing it, too?

I was being awful judgy again. Not a good look or feel. It made me feel isolated from these people. Separate from them. Like I was better than they were. Let he who hath no sin cast the first stone. It was not very becoming. Not a good start to an endeavor that I felt God had purposely set me to. Glancing skyward, I reminded God about my heart.

A fight started somewhere off to my right and the bulk of the crowd rushed to the spectacle, clearing the line to the arena gates. I handed a staffer my ticket which he scanned with something that looked like a cell phone. He stared at me for a long time with a look of either concern or confusion.

"You sure you're at the right place, pops?" he asked, handing me back my ticket.

I made my way in and the task before me seemed overwhelming. One time a group of us from the church had gone to a cleanup for fire damaged homes in the foothills of the Sierras. A mission trip sort of thing. The devastation lay everywhere. The rubble and debris and destruction. An absence of hope. And we didn't know where to start. There was plenty of work right in front of us, but what did you do first? Where to even begin.

I saw a young guy off by himself. As by himself as he could be in this crowd. I took a deep breath and went over next to him. He looked up from his phone at me.

"Hey, how's it going?" I asked.

"What?" he half yelled back. The noise was that bad. And the "music" hadn't even started yet.

I leaned in closer and half yelled myself, "I said, 'How's it going?'"

He looked me up and down. I tried to smile a bit. To seem friendly.

"Get lost, man," he said and turned and walked away.

That went well.

I shut my eyes and tried to drown out the noise. To focus. To listen to any heavenly advice, if it was forthcoming, but nothing came. What was I doing here? Had God sent me or was the phone call and the ticket and all that just some big coincidence?

I didn't really believe that. No, that was too many things that had to fall into place to make this happen. Jesus himself said that He was going to give me a platform. And that it would be difficult. And that I was to follow Him. Was this harder than going to the cross? Did He not die for all of these people here just as He had for me?

Did I really believe that?

You know, sometimes, every once in a great while, you can literally feel the Holy Spirit build inside you. It had only happened to me a few times over my life. Usually when deep in prayer. I mean a real prayer like I'd had in my office the other day. Or when you see God working in the world. Sometimes you can actually feel the Spirit inside you come to life. It usually happened with some mountain top experience and this was anything but that, but right then, with my eyes closed surrounded by a bunch of people that seemed very far away from God, I felt the Spirit. Felt it uncontrollably like a shiver on a cold morning.

In that moment I knew I did believe that Jesus wanted these people to know about Him. That He loved them and I should do the same. My heart went out to those people around me and I also believed right then that this was no accident and that He had indeed sent me here.

I felt excitement and calm. A sense of peace knowing that He was in control. That His will was being done here. I felt a smile starting to spread over my face even as my whole body started to shake with the blasts from distant speakers.

I opened my eyes and the noise of the evening descended on me again, but I looked out into the crowd with a renewed vision. My hand no longer shook.

Right then the lights went out and a huge blast of electric guitar came from the stage, so loud it hurt my ears and caused me to jump back, startled. I bumped into a guy behind me and his beer poured on my shirt. But he didn't care. As laser lights came on from the center of the arena, the guy threw up his hands and yelled along with the rest of the crowd.

The show had started.

***

The main stage, or platform if you will, sat in the middle of the arena. Four gigantic screens hung above it that were fed by video cameras which I assumed resided high up in the building and gave even people in the grandstand type seating a view of what was going on. A drum solo was blaring as the lights from the stage floor and from the overhead scaffolding went through the crowd and the band members of Lucifer took their spots. I could feel every beat of the drum reverberating through my entire body.

There was no seating on the ground level, just a swarm of bodies, most with their hands in the air yelling and screaming. The fans filled every inch of space all the way up to the platform and movement was only accomplished by sliding through people. My arms and elbows rubbed on other people's appendages as I moved through the crowd. Moving to where, I really didn't know.

I tried to grab onto that Spirit-filled feeling from moments ago, but the sound and the people fought it back. A group herded closer to the stage and somehow I was gathered up in their midst, heading towards the platform. Like a school of minnows heading to the shark's mouth.

The band went into their first song. Many people banged their heads up and down with the rhythm of the beat. Feet stomped. Hands stayed aloft. Quite frankly, I was overwhelmed. And terrified.

I wanted to go off again and regain my composure. I wondered how I could spread any message, much less the very personal one of repentance and salvation that I wanted to share with someone, anyone, here. Conversation of any sort would be futile. There was no way to hear or be heard over the crescendo of sound and music attacking my ears.

My senses were overloaded. Doubt assaulted my mind. My heart raced. Or was that the bass?

Despite my earlier reassurance, I was having a real hard time seeing God's hand in this.

After an eternity where I only understood the occasional word, often about death and loss and violence, the song ended. The crowd erupted, but at least the beating of the drum had stopped. I could almost think again. My pounding heart was now differentiated from the massive drum set in center stage.

"Hello, Bakersfield!" the voice of the lead singer yelled, his voice raspy and excited. "What fun we will have tonight! Tonight, you get to hang out with Lucifer!"

Everyone pointed up to the huge screens above the band. The cameras were sweeping the crowd and people tried to figure out if they were on the big screen or not. But how could you tell the difference between yourself and the thousands of other yelling and screaming people dressed in black?

A hue of light blue crossed through the camera frame and then stopped. Then it backed up, searching, until it found the blue again. The frame stopped on some poor sap who stood out like a mole on someone's face. Some dumb pastor who thought this'd be a good idea.

People hollered and pointed some more. A guy close to me laughed, clapping me on the shoulder and aimed his arm past my head to show me myself, giant sized, up on the monitor. Even the lead singer of the band was looking and pointing now.

The drummer hit a couple beats to start off the next song, but the lead singer held up his hands and said, "Wait. Hold on. Check it out."

He pointed a tattooed arm up to the large overhead screen. "That guy there. Is that the guy?"

The crowd roared and screamed.

"Get that dude up here!"

Somehow, the sea of people parted between me and the platform. A tiny maze through the crowd. Everyone was all smiles and yelling and clapping me on the back and spilling beer on me and blowing smoke in my face. I don't know if I walked or was pushed that direction, but suddenly I was at the edge of the stage where two security guys hoisted me up.

The lead singer came to me, staring, and said, "Dude, you are him!" The crowd roared again.

The singer was joyfully incredulous. "You're the guy from YouTube. The one in the liquor store with the gun pointing at your head."

Murmurs in the crowd now as recognition took hold. The video had been a big deal briefly. I saw enough cell phones pointing right at me now to know that this could be even bigger.

The guy held a microphone to my mouth, looking for some sort of response. His guitar was draped across his back and with the hand not holding the microphone he made a gun out of his hand and pointed it at my head. My heart was beating even harder than before. I was sweating. I thought I might pass out. Or vomit. Hopefully not both, but maybe.

That sense of calm and peace was still at the back of my mind. I was almost as scared as I had been in Marcos' liquor store. It was just a different sort of terror now. And I knew this was it. This was what Jesus had been talking about. I didn't know what He planned to do right here, but it was going to be big. This would reach so many people who needed to hear it. He would put the words in my mouth. Righteous words.

The doubt again. He would put the words in my mouth, wouldn't He?

I looked at the microphone, then the singer. He had a big spike through his nose. A cartoon Satan tattoo peeked over his collar on his neck. I leaned in towards the microphone and said, "Yeah, I'm that guy."

The crowd roared and the singer clapped his hands like this was just too much fun.

Then he came back over to me. "Wait man, aren't you a preacher or something?"

I smiled nervously, looking out over the crowd. "Yeah, I'm that guy also." So far my speech was riveting.

He laughed and howled and the crowd followed suit. He clapped his hands on his knees, caught his breath, and said, "Man, that was insane what you did in that store. It's crazy that you're here. And didn't you say you met Jesus? That he said you were to face that dude?"

"Well, kind of, but…" He took the microphone from my face before I could continue.

"Man, I tell you what." He looked at me with a grin. "You know what this is right? You know what this band is called?"

I said, "Yes, I know. But Jesus said He'd give me a platform."

He snaked the mic away again and pandered to his crowd. They thundered again. He said, "Oh, we got us a platform here. But it ain't no Jesus platform." The crowd ate it up.

"Alright, preacher man. You're up on the platform. What you got?"

He handed me the microphone this time. I was cleared to say what I wanted. How silly of me to worry about not being able to talk to anyone because of the noise. How unfaithful to doubt why He had brought me here. I was worried about one guy standing on his own, but Jesus had seen fit to let me talk to everyone. All at once too. Very efficient.

I held the microphone to my face and it trembled in front of me. I licked my lips and squinted past the blinding stage lights out into the crowd. The singer looked at me with amusement and the crowd quieted.

It wasn't until I watched the video myself that I really knew what I said. It's all sort of a blur. That exact moment at least. But I set forth the gospel. Maybe my Bible knowledge paid off. Maybe Christ did indeed put the words in my mouth.

I said,

> *"All have sinned and fall short of the glory of God.*
>
> *The wages of sin is death, but the gift of God is eternal life in Christ Jesus our Lord.*
>
> *Your iniquities have separated you from your God;*
>
> *Your sins have hidden His face from you,*
> *so that He will not hear.*
>
> *For God so loved the world that He gave His one and only Son, that whoever believes in Him shall not perish but have eternal life.*
>
> *For even the Son of Man did not come to be served, but to serve, and to give his life for many.*
>
> *While we were still sinners, Christ died for us."*

I stopped then and felt a small breeze kiss the back of my neck and I looked out on the crowd. Staring at me as the words pierced their souls.

Quiet. Everyone quit stirring. The lights and lasers stopped their chaotic sweeping of the masses. The harvest was plentiful, but the workers were few.

At least, that's how it felt. Then a beer can came from somewhere and almost hit my head. Like a switch being flipped, the quiet disappeared and the roar erupted back, louder than it had been the whole night. But there were no celebratory overtures in this noise. No, these cries were of anger.

And hate.

More beer flew onstage and I dodged it the best I could. The lead singer came to me and snatched the microphone, glaring at me, and bumping his chest into mine, backing me up to the edge of the platform.

He yelled into his own mic, the one attached around the back of his ear, to his adoring public. It was just like the one I wore on Sundays. "That the best you got, preacher man?"

His arms shot out and gave me a violent shove to my chest and I reeled off the stage. Or platform. Or Satanic altar. Whatever you want to call it.

Instead of hitting the ground, however, I was caught by a mob of outstretched hands. They cradled my entire body and the sea of arms started taking me back away from the stage. My arms and legs splayed outstretched and my face looked heavenward as the mob absconded me to the outer edge of the crowd. Laser lights screamed overhead as the electric guitars started in deep and the drums came to life once more. I bounded up and down violently, like a leaf caught in a rapid as rough hands carried and jabbed and punched as the current carried me away.

At the outer edge of the ground level crowd, I ran out of hands and hit the ground. A guy kicked at me yelling to get out. To leave. I lay in a puddle of spilled beer and who knows what else and finally collected myself enough to stand up and work my way towards an exit.

I stumbled away as the music raged everyone on. There were sneers and more cups of beer thrown my direction. I started running. Laughter wafted up behind me as I finally reached the exit gate.

The same guy who scanned my ticket when I came in was still there. His was the only halfway sympathetic face I'd seen all evening.

"I tried to tell you, man."

***

The walk through the parking lot was much less intense, though not without its share of expletives thrown my way. I got to the Ranger and climbed in, afraid that a gang of Lucifer fans would surround the vehicle and that I'd have to ram my way through. I started the truck and the headlights mercifully illuminated a clear path. I put it in gear and pulled out.

How would Christ have handled that? How would He have felt right now? As He drove His Ranger away from the deranged scene? Would He have felt love and joy and peace? Could He have possibly felt kindness and goodness? And would His faith be intact and would He be in control of Himself?

Of course, He would have. Or He would have converted that whole damn crowd. Great, now I was swearing. But He was Jesus Christ, the Son of the living God. I was Bob. Just Bob.

As I drove through the city, I fought mightily with myself. With my internal humiliation and anger. And the fear. At stop lights I wouldn't look at other cars. Just two hands on the wheel and eyes straight ahead.

Traffic lights gave way to stop signs and then to long stretches of two-lane roads heading away from Bakersfield, rolling past orchards and crop fields. It seemed more peaceful, but the turmoil inside me did not dissipate. Doubt attacked. The memory of feeling the

Spirit in me, even in the midst of all that commotion, fell away like a feather on the breeze. Had it ever really been there?

As I got closer to Lamont, I thought about calling Mary or Dave, but a sheriff's car passed going the opposite direction and I decided I better concentrate on driving and get home. I had so much spilled beer on me that I smelled like a brewery and I had a feeling the truth may not get me out of going for a ride in the backseat of a police cruiser. Not to mention there was already enough talk around town about me.

I finally turned onto our street and made the corner into our driveway, the porch light welcoming me back. Only then did my anger start to quell. Just a tad. Mary could do that.

Even though it was eleven o'clock, she was still up on the couch waiting for me. I would have expected her to be curled up with a book, but instead she had the TV on. She hopped up to come give me a hug, but I stopped her short and, before she could protest, I saw recognition in her face as her nose crinkled due to the aroma coming from my clothes.

She settled for gently putting a hand to my shoulder.

"I'm sorry, baby," she said.

I felt my eyes get misty and I fought back a tear. The love I saw in her eyes contrasted with the hate I had seen just an hour ago, and I just couldn't help it.

A commercial ended on the TV screen and the eleven o'clock news started up and guess who the lead story was?

"I'm tired of seeing you in the news," Mary said.

8

My alarm went off the next morning way too early. Dragging myself out of bed, the thoughts of last night immediately sprung to mind. Maybe it had been a dream, I thought to myself. The smell of stale beer oozed up from the dirty clothes hamper, shattering the hopeful delusion.

I crawled through the routine of getting ready for church. There was still a sermon to give and a flock to lead. Even dejected pastors had to get in front of the congregation every week. Thinking about last week's sermon didn't help my mood any.

I sat down with my Bible and my sermon notes and a cup of coffee in a chair by our living room window. But instead of going over things for the morning service, I caught myself gazing at the lighting sky in the east as the sun tried to push its rays through the ever-present haze that lay upon the San Joaquin Valley. I supposed it was better than the fog.

Even in the normalcy of the view, I could still see a creator looking back at me. Trying to reassure me as I tried to reassure myself that He did indeed love me. That this wasn't some sort of fun torture He was putting me through for His amusement.

Mary was now up and rummaging around in the kitchen. She came out with her own cup of coffee and stood behind me, looking out the window.

"Nice morning," she said.

I grunted.

"You feeling any better?" she asked.

"Not particularly."

She leaned down and kissed me. "I'll get some breakfast going for you."

She left me to my preparations. Or my broodings. Whichever.

***

I walked into the church around eight. No one was there yet, but soon the worship team would be arriving to go through the songs for the morning. Dave would get there probably about half an hour before the service and we would pray beforehand for the worship that day and for the congregation. We'd probably do our fair share of praying for the pastor as well.

Sure enough, around eight forty-five, I heard just what I expected. Rummaging around and then muffled guitar notes as instruments were tuned. The "check, check" as Tyler, our sound guy, got things fired up.

I hid in my office, and no one came to bother me. I was embarrassed to go out and see them, and they were probably just as embarrassed to see me. Lovely way to spend the day.

I struggled to go over my notes, but it was too hard to concentrate. The office phone rang and gave me a heck of a jolt because it never rang, especially not on a Sunday before the service. I answered, half expecting to hear Elmira Sanchez telling me she wouldn't be coming to a church that had a pastor who went to these heathen music concerts. Instead, it was some guy who sounded drunk going on about how he talked with Jesus too and how we should praise God for His intervention in our lives. Then just background noise and I think the guy vomited as he held the phone away from his ear. I hung up.

THORNS

The worship team started into one of the morning's songs as a ray of sun peeked through my little window. The song's words were indecipherable, but I knew the tune. Knew the song. The melody was enough. It brought a mood change upon me and I could even feel a smile starting to crease the corners of my mouth.

What did I expect? Of course it was going to be hard. He told me it would be hard. But I was doing God's work and that did fill me with joy. I decided right then to be a little more intentional in doing what He had set before me. Spread His word? You got it. No matter what it entailed. Because just like I hadn't thought the liquor store was the end of things, I didn't think that concert was either. Who was I to put limits on how far He wanted to take this?

My sermon notes stared up at me from my desk. Daring me. I sat down and went over them again, and this time they didn't seem too bad. You know what, they weren't bad at all. I felt a clarity about the Word. About the parable. I had done the evangelizing last night, but today I was pastoring. I was growing His sheep. We were going to work on their soil today. See if we could make it more fertile.

There was a light knock on my door.

I looked at my watch and saw it was way too early for Dave. My hands started to tremble a little bit, and the excitement began ramping up. I couldn't stop myself from straightening out the notes on my desk and checking the collar on my shirt. I was ready and eager.

I stood up as the door opened. A quick jolt of panic. *Maybe I should get down on my knees? Or take off my shoes or something?*

But it was Dave.

"Oh, it's you."

PART TWO: ROCKY GROUND

9

Dave looked all giddy when he stepped in, but my welcome toned that down.

"I hope you do better than that during your office hours," he said, closing the door behind him.

"Sorry, Dave. I thought you were —" I didn't know what to say, really.

"Hey, I get it. You thought you'd get Jesus again. I can play second fiddle. I just wanted to get here early. You know, in case you needed to talk about things. Talk about last night."

Dave would drop whatever he was doing to help someone out, even if it was just listening. Like he'd done many times for me. Like he'd done for that greasy jeans guy last week. It tugged at my conscience a bit that I hadn't thought about that guy at all. A lost sheep dropped on our doorstep, and I hadn't given him a second thought all week.

Well, it should be on my mind. "Dave, first, tell me about that guy from last week. The one you talked with after service. What was his name?"

"Phil," Dave said. "Yeah, I haven't heard from him or seen him around town since last week. I didn't see him outside this morning either." That was all he said, but from past experience, I knew Dave had tried to find the guy. Probably drove around and asked the homeless shelter about him.

But Dave was a guy I could be open with. He was my friend, but more so, he was an elder in this church and he took the job seriously. "Don't let the question fool you. I haven't thought about the guy all week. I just thought I should have been."

He put on his fatherly half smile. "Hey, Bob, don't let it bother you. You've had a lot going on. Dodging bullets. Going to concerts. You know, pastor stuff."

Good old Dave. He could always get me to laugh. "Yeah, I guess."

"But, Bob, has it been hard on you? I guess it would be when the Savior of the world asks you to do something, but I hadn't thought of it that way."

"It's just..." I looked around the room, like one of the books on my shelf would help me with the words. "It's just hard. First, hard to know what exactly He wants. For someone that comes to visit, He doesn't exactly say just what He means. The concert thing was..." I trailed off.

"Yeah, I saw the news footage. I was going to call, but figured you had enough calls to go around."

I let out a big sigh as I thought of all of the missed calls and texts and emails that I had ignored since last night.

"The concert," I said, as if those words were sufficient to explain it.

"Pretty bad, huh?"

I settled into my chair. "Yeah. Parts of it, I guess. You know, there were times where I so felt the Spirit at work. And a moment when I thought that that whole place was all the sudden going to come to Christ. And then, BAM. Nothing but hate. And beer. You would think with how expensive the beer was people wouldn't be so flippant with throwing it around."

"Well, I doubt they threw full ones."

I gave him a look.

But I went on anyway. "Then to just be shot down, like you had zero impact. Like you maybe solidified those people's ideals even more. And then I felt humiliated, and I feel bad for feeling that way because it must just be my pride rearing up, but it was so ... disheartening."

Dave went into full eldering mode. "Bob, think about Abraham and when God promised that he would have a family that would carry on. That his line would keep going. And somehow Abraham thought that God wanted him to have a son through Hagar. I suppose he wasn't humiliated when Isaac came along, but sending Ishmael out into the wilderness couldn't have been nice."

"So, you think he didn't want me to go to the concert?" I wasn't seeing his point.

"No. I guess what I'm getting at is that even when God speaks directly to you, you still have to move forward and do something the best you know how. And it can be hard." He had a faraway look starting up, which usually meant he was thinking about one of his Africa trips.

"I suppose what I'm going through pales a bit compared to having to send your son away."

He came back to earth. "I don't mean to poo-poo what you're experiencing, Bob. Just that it would be hard. Maybe Abraham wasn't the best example. I suppose that's why you're the pastor."

He leaned back in his own chair. I could hear more noise than usual coming from outside my office doors. A lot of scuffling and murmurs of voices that were indistinct. People roaming about.

"Well, I figured that this had to be hard. I wanted to make sure you were good."

So much of pastoring and guiding a church is wondering if you're doing the right thing. Yes, we're always praying and asking God for guidance. Asking that His will absolutely be done the way He wants it to. But you still had to make decisions and interpretations and instill things into the church and the service that were up to you. You had to do it, because you couldn't just sit around waiting for some divine revelation. In that regard, Dave's Abraham analogy wasn't half bad.

I smoothed the pages of my sermon. "You know, Dave, I am good. Really good, actually. I'm pumped up. That concert thing, as an experience, wasn't pleasant, but Christ sent me on this mission. I don't think He's done either. So, I'm going in full bore. Whatever He needs me to do."

Dave's giddiness started to reemerge. "That's awesome, Bob. What better answer could I hope for in my pastor."

It wasn't a show, either. Once my mind was set, then it was eagerness. Ready to go. How long had it been since I'd felt this way before worship? And to think, just last week I thought I was the worst pastor the world had ever encountered.

"I'm even digging my new sermon now. Much better than last week," I said.

"Great, so you've had time to work on a sermon? You're starting a new series, right?"

I held up my notes. "Yeah. Of course, I had to explain it to Jesus."

"What?"

"Not explain it, but He wasn't as familiar with the parable of the soils as I would have hoped."

"Is that bad?"

"Well, He did admit it was a good one before He left."

"Hmm" Dave said, looking back towards the door. "Well, you hear all that ruckus out there?"

I eyed him suspiciously. "Yeah…"

"It's a full house today." He looked back at me. "Parking lot's full. Standing room only."

He lowered his voice, like it was a big secret. "There are three TV news vans out there, Bob."

I looked at my watch and stacked my notes. "Well, at least no pressure."

THORNS

He put his hand on my shoulder and we gave a prayer for the service and for the congregation. Dave told our God that he didn't know what was going on, but he was confident that He did. I tried to bolster my own confidence in that statement. I found it hard to concentrate with the commotion outside.

***

He was right. The place was packed. I have never been a part of a worship service that had so much buzz and energy. The regulars were in their usual spots and singing extra loud. Really putting on a show. Was it for show or was I being a party pooper? Maybe this was what happened when Jesus reached down and jabbed a community and I was just jealous I hadn't done it. That ego thing again. Still, how could their soil have improved so much in the last 24 hours? The last week?

As the last song played, I prayed for myself. That I would be humble and just look to serve these people how God would have me do it. I prayed as hard as I could at that moment that the words that came out of my mouth would be the ones that He would have me deliver. That the Spirit would be in control of this service and not some prideful guy named Bob. That Bob wouldn't put on his own show.

I started to hope … no believe … that maybe He had placed this opportunity right here for the world to see. To hear His word delivered through me.

I clamored up to the pulpit and found I was nervous. I hadn't been nervous up here in a long time. I willed my hands not to shake as I placed my notes on the lectern and adjusted the earpiece microphone to my mouth.

I took it in for a moment. People actually had their phones up taking pictures or videos. A TV crew was set up in the back. Should I address that?

Instead, I said, "Did they cancel the playoffs or did someone see Jesus?"

That got us off to a good laugh and then things fell into place. I went through my sermon, but only had to glance at my notes every once in a while. I did touch on what I had been through because it was the elephant in the room, so why not get it out there, but after that it was just the sermon.

It was a pretty darn good one, too. We talked about our farming community and the value of good soil. And if you wanted a good crop, you better have good soil. I'd hit this parable before at some point, I'm sure, but the plan was to dive deep into it this time, going through each soil type over the next couple weeks.

I even got a couple "amens" from the crowd. Appropriately timed, too.

***

Greeting time at the end was much livelier than the week before. Everyone wanted to stop and shake hands or hug or tell me what a good sermon it was. No one tried to sneak away. It was all back slapping and smiles. Some days it was good to be a pastor.

Even George Liston wasn't in a hurry.

"Great sermon, pastor," he said pumping my hand, Lila on his arm.

"Thank you," I beamed. "Where's Matthew at today?"

Lila's eyes went to her feet. George said, "Oh, you know these kids, pastor. He went to some concert last night. Couldn't get him out of his room this morning."

They went off and my mood threatened to dampen. The concert.

But before I could get too sulky, a reporter had a microphone in my face. "Pastor Bob, how does church feel today after the events of last night?"

I was caught off guard by the suddenness. And maybe by the microphone. My last encounter with a microphone shoved in my face hadn't gone all that well. I mumbled a couple of "uhms" and "uhs" trying to figure out what to do.

There were more reporters behind this one. I took a deep breath to gather myself.

"Church was just fine, thank you. But I would rather not speak to the events of last night right now. I'm sorry." I started for my office, reporters on my tail.

"Pastor, when will we be able to see Jesus?"

"Pastor, can you comment on the investigation of the liquor store robbery?"

"Pastor, how do you respond to the people saying that this is all some stunt you've concocted due to low parishioner turnout?"

Somehow, I had the good sense to keep walking, finally arriving at my office door, and getting safely tucked away.

To their credit, the reporters let me be in peace. I tried to decompress, not to mention make sense of all that had happened. The robbery, the concert, the visit by Jesus, and his requests of me. Did Jesus make requests?

I turned on the jazz station to its perfunctory role of background noise and leaned back in my chair. I closed my eyes and the tension slowly left my body. My doubts and fears and humiliations slowly melted and the budding excitement picked up again.

Was this what Jesus had been trying to say to me? That these difficulties would lead to this? An awakening? Sure, Lamont Community Church was just that, a little community church, but with the excitement and the media presence, was some sort of spiritual awakening right around the corner?

A revival, now? That was an interesting thought. A spiritual revival was what this country needed. Not just this country, but even little rural, conservative Lamont,

California. A revival is what I needed. Jonathan Edwards, Richard Allen, Dwight Moody... Bob Jordan?

I wanted to be humble. I prayed to be humble about it. To tell myself that it wasn't me, but Him in me that had made this come about. But I couldn't help those other thoughts from creeping in.

And it had been a good sermon today.

10

When I pulled up in our driveway, I had to go around a Channel 24 News van. I hopped out at the same time as one of the reporters from earlier today also got out. She was persistent. Her cameraman was close in tow.

"Pastor Bob, can we ask you a few questions?" At least she was not as abrupt as earlier today.

Behind her I noticed the sunset. In the valley, there seemed to always be a haze of dust in the air. Sometimes it made for the most spectacular of sunsets. Pink tonight. A brilliant pink turning into a dark blue with a couple of shadowy clouds hovering about. The weather was even nice tonight. A good evening for sitting on your porch. Unless you had the media clamoring for an exclusive.

The beauty of the horizon, however, was also a reminder. It was late. I almost never came home this late on a Sunday.

"I'm sorry," I said to the reporter. "But I am still not going to speak on the things that God has been doing. I'm going to spend the evening with my wife and son. Quietly."

It felt a little rude, but I did not wait for a response. I just went inside the house.

The smell of dinner cooking overwhelmed my nostrils, bringing my mood back to the good side.

I couldn't see Mary, so I hollered, "Smells great, Babe."

Mary came out from the kitchen and gave me a kiss. "Good thing you finally got home. Dinner just got done. I was worried maybe you stopped by the liquor store again."

"Thanks," I said, feigning hurt.

James came running down the hall and I crouched down to meet his approach.

I hugged him tight. "Hey, little man, how was Sunday school today?"

"It was good. We got Rice Krispies Treats."

"Ah, yes," I said with the air of an all-knowing sage. "The way to young spiritual enlightenment is always through sugar. It's in the Bible somewhere."

"Daaad," he whined. Then his eyes got big and his eyebrows rounded. "Is that what Jesus told you?"

The pastor, who always had something to say, was rendered silent on this one. I looked at Mary, but her return stare held no sympathy. How to explain this to my ten-year-old son? I'm sure the kids at school had been teasing him about it, but I had successfully avoided the issue all week.

"I was kidding, James. Rice Krispies Treats are not in the Bible. Although there is a thing called mana. Have you learned about that?"

He looked at me strangely, tumbling the unfamiliar word over in his mind. "No. Did Jesus bring you some?"

I decided I had avoided the conversation long enough. I looked over my shoulder. Mary was still listening. She wanted to see how I would handle this, too.

I picked up James under the arms and set him on the couch, taking a seat next to him. His eyes beamed up to mine and I felt his adoration piercing into my soul, beckoning me to share the secrets of life with him. To be a father.

"Listen, buddy, I'm going to be serious. I'm sure the kids might have been teasing you at school about me meeting Jesus."

His brow furrowed at this, a stern expression coming over his face. "Just Tommy Chambers."

"Well, I tell you what. I don't know how or even exactly why, but Jesus came and saw me last week. And He told me things. But they were all things that are already in our Bible. Things that maybe I had just forgotten about. Nothing new. Just a reminder that there are a lot of people out there who need to hear about Him. And He wants me to tell them."

His eyebrows remained downcast as his eyes went away from mine. He was thinking about what I'd told him. He was still young and, in his mind, his father was the bastion of truth. What I said was the gospel to him. Poor kid.

Finally, he looked back up. "Should I tell Tommy Chambers about Jesus?"

I let a big breath out. "Uhm. That's a hard one. You could tell Tommy about Jesus. But if he doesn't want to hear it, don't push it."

He continued to look at me, but I didn't know what else to say.

I tussled his hair instead. "Anything else?" I asked.

"Can I watch TV?"

I laughed out loud at that. "Sure, buddy."

I looked behind me again, but Mary had left. I went to the kitchen and found her looking in the oven.

She stood and went to the window by the front door and peeked through the blinds. "I'm glad you got by the news lady."

I took her in my arms and gave her a tight hug and just held her. Mary. Always my support. Lord knows I need it. Even if she thought I was loony.

"Sorry I'm so late," I said into her ear.

"No problem. You've got a lot happening right now." She pecked my cheek. "C'mon, before it gets cold."

We sat down to a dinner of lasagna and salad. I said grace and we dug in.

"How did Sunday School go for you?" I asked Mary as we ate.

She dabbed her mouth with a napkin. "Fine. You were a hot topic, though. All those kids were talking about 'Pastor Bob at the Lucifer concert'. They played it over and over on their phones."

"I guess that was probably disturbing."

"Not too bad, really. You know, in all the news clips, they just show you getting things thrown at you. At least some of these online deals have you speaking. At least those kids are hearing that part."

"Did you tell the people at the concert about Jesus, Dad?"

James had pasta sauce all over his face. "Yeah, I tried."

I hadn't realized that the news had edited out my message from the concert. I suppose it didn't surprise me. What gets the most views? Some pastor saying pastor things or some pastor getting beer thrown at him?

We ate in silence. I wiped up some marinara with a piece of bread.

James got done and he put his dishes in the sink. I eyeballed him to make sure he rinsed his plate and he did. Mary sent him off to take a bath.

"I hear the sermon went well today," Mary said.

"Yeah, it was good. You know what? The whole thing was good. Except the reporters. That was just weird."

"You're good with the concert thing now? You were pretty bummed last night."

"I was. And scared. But now I'm excited too, you know? I mean, I think Christ is going to do something really special at our church. I'm starting to get pumped about it, honestly. I'm starting to feel inspired instead of just so dispirited. I think I'm starting to feel more like Paul and less like Jonah."

She didn't say anything. Evidently, she wasn't that inspired.

I put down my fork. "I'm sorry, Mary. Is it bad for you?"

She looked away. "No, Bob. It's fine for me. A couple comments at the hospital, but whatever. But it must be hard on you. And stressful."

"A little. At the concert it seemed horrible, but even that, only a day past, seems not that bad anymore."

She moved the last little bit of lasagna around on her plate, the metal fork making a light screeching noise against the porcelain. The implications of what I'd said bothered her more than she wanted to let on.

"So," she said. "You don't think it's done? Whatever it is?"

"I'm sorry, but no. I think He still has some things to do. I wish I could share my excitement with you, babe. I think our God has some big things coming up."

We both carried our dishes to the sink. I grabbed another bit of lasagna out of the pan with my fork. I thought she'd teasingly slap at my hand, but she didn't. I had not persuaded her and I felt there were things still unsaid. Not the way to end the day.

I started rinsing the dishes to put them in the washer. She bumped me out of the way. "I'll get these. You better get going."

I wiped my hand on the towel and looked at her with my head cocked to the side. "Going where?"

She placed the plates in the rack. "The trustee's meeting. They got to have their pastor there. Probably a long one tonight."

Oops. The trustees' meeting. I'd forgotten all about it.

***

Ever the punctual pastor, I made it on time. Only thanks to Mary, of course. But, hey, I'd married her, so good on me. We gathered in the small conference room outside my office. Everyone was there tonight. A rarity. There were six trustees for our little church, including Dave. I made up the seventh. The deciding vote I liked to joke. We had no need for a deciding vote as everything was unanimous. Maybe not at first on all issues of the church and its finances, but sooner or later we found unity or we simply moved on.

There was more than the usual amount of chit-chat before the meeting. Lots of smiles. A full church will do that for its board. I didn't particularly care for meetings on Sundays, but it was only once a month. Tonight though? I wanted to get into things. To see if everyone was starting to feel the excitement that I did. We got seated and I opened the meeting with a prayer.

Usually, myself or Gwenith Sheridan, our board secretary, would have formulated an agenda, but Gwen hadn't and I had barely remembered the meeting, so it was off the cuff. That turned out to be okay, however, because everyone pretty much just wanted to talk about what had been happening in my life.

Frank Bowler led the opening salvo. "So, Pastor, we've all heard this craziness about you chumming it up with Jesus. I mean, Bob, that is pretty far out there."

His eyebrows raised. A slight smirk. Like I was about to let him in on the big joke.

"I'm sorry, Frank. And I know how out there it seems. I wish I'd kept that to myself, but it happened. I met Jesus. Right there," I said, indicating my office door behind me.

Gwen was sitting next to me and set a hand on my forearm. "Yes, dear, that's fine. You mean in a spiritual or prayerful way you've been talking to the Lord?"

Gwen had been the board secretary for a long time. I mean, a long time. Since before I was here. She liked to call me "dear."

"No, Gwen, like a human being came in claiming to be Jesus Christ. And it was Him."

I went over the whole story with the trustees. Something more than newsclips and church gossip. I started with Him coming right in my door. The proofs He'd given me. Then the real proof of the liquor store robbery. The concert.

Gwen set her pencil down. Frank cleared his throat. I think they all thought that somehow it was being misconstrued in the media. I think they all felt like Frank had. Like it was a joke or a stunt or something.

Bill Matthews, our treasurer, finally chimed in. "Well, the giving has certainly been off the charts this week. And I haven't looked at the online giving today, but it was ten-fold the normal when I checked yesterday." It had always been my experience that heavy giving made for a happy trustees' board.

"Yeah, that's great," I said. "But didn't you guys feel that excitement this morning? The love in the worship? I mean, couldn't you feel the Spirit working today? I don't think this is a flash in the pan fad sort of deal. I think God is trying to do something powerful for His kingdom here. With us. Through us."

Frank scanned the group. "That's fine, Bob. If that's the story, that's fine. It was exciting today. I've been on high the whole day."

I raised my hands in despair. "Do you guys think I would go to some Satanic concert on a whim? Or that I would stand in front of some gang kid with a gun because of a vague premonition?"

Ceasar Silva added his two cents. "Hey, I was talking with Clint Jones. You know, he works for the PD in Bakersfield. He has some connection with the Sheriff's Department. They said every one of the bullets they took out of that gun had a dimple in the primer where the firing pin had hit it. They even loaded one back in the gun and shot it at some ballistic gel, and it went off."

Ceasar always had some sort of story like this. Usually, it bordered on gossip and I would have to gently move him another direction. This one intrigued me, however. I hadn't heard it yet.

"Okay. So, the pastor pulled off some sort of miracle. Maybe he did hear from God. But that Jesus Himself is making house calls? Well, you won't have those big crowds for long with that. I don't think God is bringing the next revival through Lamont." Frank sat back, crossing his arms.

The rest of the group talked back and forth but I tried to block them out and focus on regaining my composure. This is understandable, I told myself. If I had read about some crazy pastor from California getting visits from Jesus, what would I think? I stole a glance at Dave, but he just grinned back at me, enjoying the show.

He did finally attempt to come to my rescue and get the group on a better path. "Hey gang," he said. "Maybe the sermons will keep these folks filling the seats. That was a pretty good one today, Bob."

They did all seem to agree on that, which was good. A pastor always likes to hear that his sermon is good. Especially when he thinks people are being honest about it.

"It was good," Bill Matthews said. I could hear a "but" coming. "But it was pretty heavy on Scripture."

"Yeah," Ceasar said. "I was talking with my cousin after. You know, he works over at Alegre Farms? He and his wife thought maybe it was a little preachy. Talking about the soil and tilling it and how some soil was just not going to take any seed. At least not without some help."

"Yes, preachy is a good word," said Frank. "And this talk about the kingdom and the evil one. You know, there were those cameras in there, Bob. Maybe we should tone it down a bit."

I tried to get us back on track. On track of what this meeting was supposed to be about, which was the church finances and how to spend the money given by our people. What needed fixing at the church? And could we afford a new DVD player for the kindergarten room? We never really got into my sermons too much in here. Especially not to the degree that I was being told to tone it down. Something like that might be appropriate for a meeting between me and Dave as a pastor and his elder, but that wasn't the function of the trustees.

We did go over a few financial decisions, but it always led back to the sermon and how to keep people coming back. Pretty soon, it didn't seem that I even heard a word being said. I saw Dave yawn and I looked at my watch. 9:45. Our budget meetings didn't even go this long.

"Okay, everyone," I said. "Hey, it's late. But let's leave at least being thankful that we had a good day today. A powerful day where a lot of new faces got to see our church and see us worship and to maybe glimpse a little of what He can do in our lives. Let's close it with that."

That seemed to appease everyone. I closed us out with a prayer of thanks. Everyone shuffled out. Dave clapped me on the shoulder, reassuringly. I stayed slumped in my chair for five minutes in silence, then finally hit the lights and went home.

11

For the second Monday in a row, I went into my office at the church. No TV crews or huge crowds of people. Just an empty parking lot.

The computer beeped when I turned it on. I went to the kitchen to get a bottle of water while the archaic machine warmed up. I sat down at my desk and looked at the blinking red light on the answering machine. I was going to have to figure out something with all of these messages. Maybe we could afford a secretary for me with our newfound riches. Maybe I should just delete them all as they came in.

I hit play. It was another reporter looking for an interview. But this time it wasn't The Bakersfield Californian print paper and not even Channel 24 out of Fresno. It was Good Morning America.

I leaned back in my chair as the computer screen finally blinked to life. I ignored it and played the answering machine message again. Good Morning America. They wanted to do a piece on me for the Sunday show in two weeks. And they wanted to interview me in studio.

Their studio was in New York City, right? Man, the logistics of trying to make something like that happen. Finding a pastor to give a sermon on a weeks' notice. Running it past Mary. Could she go? Who would take James to school and pick him up? Did ABC pick up the airfare? Would I have to wear makeup? You always had to do that on camera, or so I'd heard.

Unfortunately, and ashamedly, the last question that came to my mind should have been the first one: was this the best for our church? Was this the best for the Kingdom and my function within it? It certainly seemed the sort of thing that God was placing in front of me lately, but my willingness to go was perhaps a bit too eager.

What would a good Christian do here? What would Mary or Dave do in this case? What would Jesus do? They'd all likely pray about it. A pastor should have been able to figure that out on his own.

So, I prayed, and even got down on bended knee. I asked God the usual questions about whether this was from Him. Did I go? Did I politely decline or just erase the message?

When finished, and with no clear-cut answers from on high, I got back into my chair. I opened up my red Bible and started in with John again. But my focus wasn't there as I read and reread the same paragraph. I caught myself looking towards the office door quite a few times, too.

I gave up, closed the book, and leaned back with my eyes closed. This would be a huge platform. Did it get any bigger? Like a building crescendo. From the robbery, to the concert, and now a national television news show? Who knows what the next step would be?

A scraping against the window drew my attention. A soft brushing from the leaves of the tree outside my office moving in a breeze. It beckoned me to come outside, which was the best idea I'd come up with yet. At least it was something different. I had a spot I could go.

***

THORNS

I pulled into the parking lot of a wetlands park just out of town. There were several cars in the lot which was actually one of the reasons I'd come here. To get away from vehicles and people. To be alone outside and seek guidance that way. Some of the biggest, or at least more heartfelt, revelations from God that I had ever personally received were from spending time outdoors alone with His word. Not counting when Jesus had actually come into my office, of course.

Most of the San Joaquin Valley had at one time been a giant marshland or wetland. Human development had created the vast expanses of farm fields and highways and homes that now sat upon the earth. The drained soil did leave behind its nourishing minerals, though, and that led to this being quite possibly the most productive farming area in the world.

The parking lot looked over a wide vista which represented, perhaps, what this landscape had been eons ago. How God had left it until humans had crafted it to their own desires. Maybe that was a negative way of looking at things. Perhaps God was pleased with how things had turned out. The soil was certainly still fertile. You could grow a good crop here.

Birds flitted about in the reeds and a pair of mud hens glided to the far end of the small water entrapment in front of me. There was a trail that went through the wetland made of wood planks and far off I could see some guy standing. Probably bird watching. Another group of people were making their way towards the parking lot.

I sat in the Ranger, taking in the landscape as the small breeze continued, gusting occasionally, and rocking the truck the slightest bit. Must be some small late spring storm coming through. Maybe we'd get a little rain out of it. There weren't many clouds, though.

The TV thing was a big deal. It was huge. Well, it could be huge. A giant platform to spread God's word.

The good news of a savior. But I didn't know if they'd just let me prattle on about whatever I wanted. Most likely the story was about the Jesus sighting.

I thought again about how I'd let that slip out during the liquor store ordeal. It made the rest of my message seem second string, but the message of what I was trying to tell people was the real story. The one I wanted to put out there. One, a flash in the pan. Quickly forgotten. The other? Life changing. Something that developed roots.

The group coming to the parking lot had reached their car and I glanced over at them. They talked happily, although I couldn't tell what words they were using. The sound was jubilant, though. They were out having a good time. One of them reached for the passenger door and I saw a neon colored bracelet on her wrist. I saw the others had the same thing.

Their car started up and the stereo started blasting out a tune before the driver could turn it down. He finally did and I could hear the raucous laughter of the group before they reversed and then pulled out of the lot. I recognized the tone of the song, too. Something I'd heard on the Christian radio station lately. I guess if kids were going to blast their radios, I'd prefer that over something from Lucifer.

I looked back out the windshield over the wetlands and stared at the shimmering strobe of sunlight flashing on the small waves made by the breeze. I hadn't made any progress on my dilemma. Do the TV spot? It matched the evangelical tone of Jesus's request of me, but I still had his flock to shepherd at the church.

I straightened up in my seat as I noticed the bird watcher heading back my direction. That profile looked familiar. The stature was right. The wooden boardwalk dipped just below my view and it looked as if the guy was walking right on the water itself. As he got closer, I started to become more sure of what I was seeing.

I got out of the Ranger and tried to focus on the figure approaching, squinting against the sun which obscured his facial features. My heart quickened. The only thing I could distinguish was that this guy also had on one of those bracelets. The neon ones that those kids had worn.

When he was twenty feet away, the emotional letdown I felt reaffirmed how excited with anticipation I had been. I said a "how's it going" to the guy to be polite as I tried to hide my disappointment. It wasn't his fault he wasn't Jesus.

He gave a generic response and was about to walk by but stopped short and turned around to face me.

"Hey, you're that pastor, right? The one who saw Jesus?"

Oh, boy. "Yeah. That's me," I said, trying to act as meek as I could. Also trying not to invite further discussion.

The guy shook my hand vigorously. "Oh, wow. Cool."

Then he held up his wrist. "Check it out, I've got one of your bracelets."

With that he went over to the other car in the lot, got in, and left.

One of my bracelets? Maybe craziness wasn't just reserved for pastors out here.

I stood in the breeze a couple minutes until I started to get a little chilly, just standing in my tee shirt. I got back in the Ranger, but didn't start it up right away. I peered out the windshield again. Finally, I turned the engine over and headed back to town. I had a little time I could spend at the office if I wanted before I had to pick up James. As I went down the main road to the church, I couldn't help but notice a lot of people had those bracelets on.

***

Back in my office I picked up the phone and dialed the number the woman had left me. I expected it to be for the studio office or the show office or whatever they called it and that I would hear from a receptionist who would then patch me through to some one's voicemail. Then they would call back and work out the details and answer my questions.

The line picked up. "Hello, this is Samantha." It caught me off guard and left me at a loss for words. Samantha Gilroy was the Good Morning America lead anchor on the weekends. The lady who led the show and interviewed the guests. She was a household name. Not that I watched Good Morning America; I had other commitments Sunday mornings. But even I knew who she was. And the voice was familiar.

"Hello?" she said again.

"Is this Samantha Gilroy?"

She didn't answer specifically but instead said with a put-out tone, "How did you get this number?" Like I was some stalker who'd derived her cell phone number through nefarious means.

"Sorry," I said, gathering my wits. "This is Bob Jordan. I'm the pastor for Lamont Community Church in California. You left me a message."

To my great relief, her tone improved immediately.

"Oh, Pastor Bob! Thank you so much for getting back to me. Good Morning America would love to have you on our show to talk about the incredible things that have been happening to you in Bakersfield."

"The concert or the liquor store?" I asked.

"Neither, although they might come up. Probably will have to because of how viral it went. But people are abuzz about your supposed encounters with Jesus." I could imagine her trademark smile beaming into the phone. *Supposed* encounter. She should be a trustee.

I told her that the meeting with Jesus was really secondary to the message I was trying to promote. I started to explain, but she interrupted saying she would love for me to tell it all on camera. She answered some of my other questions. Yes, they would cover airfare and accommodations in New York. Yes, Mary could come, but we'd have to foot the bill for that. Yes, I would have to wear makeup.

I needed to think about it. To pray about it and talk with my wife. It seemed awfully short notice, maybe two weeks was cutting it too close? How about they do some satellite feed and I didn't have to go to New York at all?

I imaged her smile disappearing, replacement by a motherly look. Like she had to explain the facts of life to me. "Pastor, we really need to do it soon. Two weeks may be too far out. It's a bit of a time crunch for us, too. But, well, how do I say this… you are a very hot story right now. These things can be short lived. The audience is abuzz about it now. But two weeks? And this is definitely an in-studio story. We'll get some background video for the lead in, but this deserves the biggest stage."

I didn't respond and so we had a few seconds of awkward silence. She said, "That's just the way the news business is, pastor. I understand you have to think about it, but I do need an answer soon. Today, if possible."

More silence on my end. "Bob," she said and I could almost feel her placing a hand delicately, reassuringly, on my arm. "Think of the platform for your message this could be."

***

Mary was opposed to the idea. She felt that I was either taking things too far or maybe too fast. Of course, she still wasn't convinced that Jesus had come to visit me, but all of these things happening made it harder for her to deny.

"Bob," she'd said, "what if this isn't what He wants you to do right now? You had the liquor store thing. I don't know if I can handle something like that again."

"Babe," I tried to be reassuring. "How can I deny what is happening? All of these opportunities falling at my feet. It can't all be coincidence."

"Kids eating Tide Pods was a thing for a while, too, Bob. It was all over the internet and the news for a while. I certainly saw enough of it in the hospital. Doesn't mean it was a good thing, much less ordained by God Himself."

I drummed my fingers on the table. Mary had always been my rock and we'd always been a team. She'd helped make the decision when I took the low paying position in Texas. She was the one who saw the opportunity here in California. But on this one? She was distant. But she hadn't had Jesus look her in the eye.

I took her hand to try and reestablish our bond. Our kinship. She didn't pull her hand away, but it was cold and clammy and she did not return the squeeze that I had given.

James thought it was great that his dad was going to be on TV. Until I told him I wouldn't be on a cartoon, but on the news. That soured him on the whole deal.

Dave thought it was crazy, but just the sort of thing that Jesus had called me to do on this crazy quest.

My prayers about it remained unanswered and no curly haired fellow came through my door to give precise direction. Left to my own devices, I called Samantha Gilroy back and told her that I would accept the invitation to go on her show.

She acted very happy and excited, but immediately went into a litany of items that had to be done. She took down my email to send me a schedule that she would coordinate to make the piece work.

The rest of the week was filled with the details of preparing for an impromptu televised Sunday morning show appearance. Basically, that meant a lot of time spent with the local ABC affiliate out of Fresno following me around and filming me to try and capture some mood and intro footage to play before the interview. A lot of staged things to show what a small-town pastor did with his day when not meeting with Jesus. Of course, they wanted to film in the office where Jesus would visit me. And they wanted some footage from Marcos's liquor store. And, yes, I had to wear makeup for these little spots as well.

I also had church business to attend to. Usually, a pastor's absence was planned out in advance, with ample time to find someone to fill the pulpit while I was away. I also had to tell the trustees what was going on, which I did through email, but they each called me in turn with questions. I answered the best that I could and apologized for the late notice, but reiterated that I thought God was doing something big in our church, in our country, and that this was a huge opportunity.

To fill the pulpit, I ended up turning to the ever-reliable Dr. William Jay. Dr. Jay was an old ex-professor but a solid Christian. He didn't come to our church much, preferring to attend another church closer to his home, but he had filled in before and was available for next Sunday's service.

When I told Dave, he was not impressed.

"Dr. Jay?" he whined.

"Yeah," I said. "What's wrong with Dr. Jay? He gives a good message."

"The message is fine, but the delivery. Well, Bill Jones won't be the only guy sleeping through the sermon."

"C'mon Dave, he can't be that bad."

"He only fills in when you're not here, so it's hard to trust your opinion on the matter."

I asked Dave if he would like to give the sermon instead. Dave decided Dr. Jay would be fine.

12

Getting the pastor nailed down early was a big help. It allowed me to concentrate on the other things I needed to do before I left for New York. I still had a sermon series to map out, but it was hard to stay focused. Most of it I had already roughly laid out. We'd gotten through the soil along the path. Next was the rocky soil. Being gone meant a gap in the series, but I couldn't see a way around it. Dr. Jay could probably handle the third soil, if I wanted, but, frankly... I didn't want that.

The Good Morning America show wasn't the only distraction, either. The idea of something even bigger continued to rattle around in my brain. I couldn't shake it. Mary's words came to me that I was going too fast. Trying to do too much.

I leaned back in my chair as I thought about Mary and how our relationship had been stretched thin lately. What if this was just the start? How would things play out between us? Jesus had said in my office that I would have to choose between my life and doing what He asked. What if...?

The line of thought was rapidly going somewhere I didn't want it to. Especially when I thought about James.

James.

Uh-oh. I looked at my watch, then hopped up and ran out to the truck. I was supposed to pick up James ten minutes ago.

J.O. THOMPSON

***

The Lamont Elementary School was small with only a handful of teachers. One of them (Mrs. Liddy, I think) stood on the steps talking with James. I parked at the curb and hopped out, offering my apologies to Mrs. Liddy. She assured me that it was not a big deal, but her eyes were accusatory. I was certainly not getting her vote for parent of the year.

James didn't care. What cares did a ten-year-old boy have?

As we drove home, I noticed a bright neon bracelet on his wrist.

"What you got there, buddy? A lot of people have those."

He held it up proudly. "It's cool dad. Tommy Chambers gave it to me."

That was a surprise. "Oh, wow. You and Tommy are pals now?"

"Not really, but he was nicer today and gave me this bracelet."

"Well, that's a start."

He shoved it in front of my face and I had to tilt my head to keep my eyes on the road. "Look, Dad, it's a bracelet about you."

With one hand I gently pushed his arm down. "Hey, buddy, I've got to see the road."

Keeping my head still, I alternated looking at the road and looking at James' wrist to focus on the bracelet. "What do you mean it's about me?"

He held it back up, at a distance, not between my eyes and the windshield.

"Look," he said.

Rotating my gaze, I was able to focus on the thing. Bright neon green mostly, but with other brightly colored shades pooled into the green. Black letters said, "PB&J."

"Peanut butter and jelly? How is that about me?"

James thought that was hilarious. Maybe not parent of the year, but comedian of the year honors were in my future. "No, Dad, not peanut butter and jelly."

I was the comedian who didn't get his own joke. "Help me out here, James."

"It means 'Pastor Bob and Jesus'."

***

A group text started going through the trustees and myself. Frank Bowler thought we needed to hold a special meeting this week. Trying to get everyone to show up to a regular meeting was hard enough, but this time, everyone was onboard to meet again this Sunday after the service. That was fine by me. I had wanted to get with them anyway to discuss next Sunday with me being gone. The tone of the text was cordial, so I didn't expect any shenanigans. The word of my impending TV appearance had made the rounds through town and everyone probably wanted to know what was up. A good church board should be concerned about their pastor going on live television.

Sunday service went fine. Maybe not with the same energy as the week before, but pretty pumped up all the same, especially for our little band of conservative congregants. My sermon was good, too. I think. Could a pastor really know if his sermon was good or not, or was its value dictated by the impact it had? Oh well, it felt good. Everyone seemed engaged. Bill Jones stayed awake the entire time.

Definitely not as packed as last week, but there were still people who had to stand in the back. Only one news crew this time. That still had me on edge, but just because I wasn't used to it. Hard to tell them no cameras when it was common knowledge I was going in front of a national camera a week from today.

I talked about deepening our roots and deepening the roots of those around us. For our agriculturally minded, I asked why they took the rocks out of the soil. It was about deep roots to withstand the elements. I saw Dave sitting in the back and thought about the different root structure between him and his wife Elena and the different turns their faiths had taken after the loss of their child.

Of course, I addressed the TV spot next week, and I tied it in to a deepening of the roots of this whole nation. We (and I made sure to refer to it as we) had a chance to share God's promise of freedom and forgiveness with the nation and I couldn't pass it up. Someone hollered something about if Jesus would show up, but I ignored it.

I spotted quite a bit of neon green in the room. Not just the bracelets, either. The color itself seemed a vehicle of the message with some bright tee shirts and one new guy in the back with a neon yellow tie. Some people still wore a suit and tie to church.

Greeting time at the end was just as joyous as the week before. Only a couple of people ran off without at least talking to someone else from the congregation. There were more back slaps and handshakes and hugs and praise for a good sermon. The Listons came out with Matthew in tow. Matthew had his head down, but I noticed no phone this time and no ear buds. He'd probably gotten them taken away or something like that. Good for George and Lila. Maybe they were using a little discipline on that kid. Helping out his root system.

All of the other trustees were seated in the conference room when I came in. Bill Mathews sat a little ways off, going over the offering from this morning and he looked pleased. Good. Pastoring 101: it's hard for a board to get after the preacher too bad when the finances are looking plentiful. It was like the "happy wife, happy life" saying.

The air was a little stuffy so I opened a window. The combination of all of these bodies in the little room, not to mention the Styrofoam cups of coffee that everyone else had, tended to make things balmy. It was church coffee so you didn't get the smell of it, just steam.

I tried to head off what I felt the biggest issue was. "Listen everyone, I'm sorry I didn't ask you all about the Good Morning America thing, but they needed an answer fast, so I did what I thought was best."

Frank Bowler, the one who had initiated this meeting, said, "Well, Bob, it would be nice to have a little heads up. Especially when you get the word from someone else and we don't know anything about it. Do you think this is best for our church?"

Occasionally, Frank and I had little tiffs. Not one of my finer qualities.

"Honestly, Frank, I didn't give a whole lot of thought about if this was good for Lamont Community Church or not." I was about to prod Frank here. And I wanted to, but I didn't want to prod so hard as to cause a big fight. "But I did think it was best for Christ's church and I let that be my deciding factor."

The room was quiet after that one. Frank's face got a little red. I had to quickly get to the reason that I also wanted this meeting.

"Listen everyone. I know a lot of you can't really get behind this idea that I saw Jesus. And I understand that. And while my actions of late have their genesis in that encounter, all the things I am doing are things that we are called to do in Scripture, not just something I came up with. Jesus did tell me that the whole world would be able to see and hear me. But is that much different than preaching the gospel to the ends of the earth?"

"It is great when God's Word can be on national, secular, television," Ceasar Silva said. "I know a guy whose cousin got on TV and his mission really took off after that." Ceasar always knew "a" guy.

Frank held up a green bracelet. "What about these, Bob? Did the church pay for these, too?"

"I don't know who started those, Frank. That wasn't my doing."

"Just someone trying to share your message?" he asked.

"I don't know."

Bill Matthews chimed in. "Probably just someone trying to make a buck off of what Bob's been doing. Even if they're a dollar a pop, I see those things everywhere."

A lot of murmuring and chatter followed that remark. The bracelets had seemed to take over the area. Ceasar knew a guy who'd counted twenty of them on a bus in Bakersfield.

I held up my hand while trying to collect my thoughts. "I don't know who gets what out of the bracelets, but I think they are a nice visual to what God's trying to do through us. Through this church for the larger body. Through these things that have been happening, the word is going around. The excitement is growing. Excitement for Jesus. Last week I told you that I thought He had real big plans that started here."

"You think bracelets is it?"

"No, not bracelets, but more than a hold up or a concert or even going on a TV show."

They looked at me expectantly. I took a breath. This was rapid acceleration for a church board.

"We have this momentum for Christ right now. Let's not let it die down. How about a big event? A revival. A big deal for the whole community."

"Oh, everyone hanging around a camp fire outside, Bob?" Frank said, jokingly.

But I was over joking. I pointed right at him. "Maybe. A lot of people and the word of God for our whole area."

More looks. More clamoring of words.

"When are we going to do that, Bob? What about the cost?" Frank, losing control again.

"We do it in two weeks. Thirteen days, actually. I'll be in New York next weekend, but the Friday after that? Why not? Why wait?"

"That's a lot to get done in two weeks, dear." Gwen said as she took notes. The ever-diligent secretary.

"I see no reason to let the fire die down. It's the reason Samantha Gilroy wants me on so soon. We wait too long and the excitement fades away."

"You didn't answer about the cost, Bob?"

I looked at Bill Matthews. "Bill, how's the giving?"

Bill took his glasses off and looked up from the checks and cash in front of him. "Well," he said, running a finger under his collar, "The finances are rather robust right now. Giving has been exceptional, especially online, which I haven't looked at yet."

I gazed at them as if to say what other proof did they need.

No murmurs this time. Just quiet. You could hear the birds chirping through the open window.

Frank looked at Dave. "Dave, what is your feeling."

It was a good question. It was obvious to everyone that Frank and I were at odds a bit. But Frank was still a smart guy. And a good guy. Even though he knew Dave and I were very tight, he also knew what we all did: that Dave was one hundred percent God's Kingdom first. Therefore, his opinion was always highly valued.

Dave leaned back in his chair. "Well, obviously a lot of doors are opening right now. The question is, who's opening them?"

That stung. Maybe Dave wasn't as gung-ho with my Jesus encounter as he'd let on. Or my excitement when we were face to face was too overwhelming. Or I was just hearing what I wanted to hear.

"There's a spot in Acts," Dave said, "where Peter and John are before the Sanhedrin or the Sadducees." Dave paused and looked at everyone in the room. "And they didn't know what to do with Peter and John because they just wouldn't shut up about Jesus. They wanted to kill them.

"But there was this old guy named Gameril or Gabriel or Gamaliel. Something like that. Anyway, do you know what he said, and ultimately what they did?"

Silence. Most people didn't know their Bible like Dave did, although I was pretty sure I knew where he was going.

"They let them go. They knew that if what John and Peter were doing was from man, then it would fail. But if it was indeed from God . . . well, then nothing could stop it anyway."

It was hard to argue with. Of course, there was a little more to the verse. Like how the other uprisings before Peter and John had ended with the death of those involved. But the point was still valid, so I kept quiet.

***

"I wished you and James could go with me," I told Mary on Friday morning. My suitcase sat next to our door, and I had the Ranger running outside to let the engine warm up. It was still dark out, the sky in the east just starting to gray off.

Mary didn't say anything. She continued making her lunch for the day. And one for James. I slouched and hung my head. Between working at the hospital and coordinating getting James back and forth to school, this meant extra work for Mary. Her attitude wasn't helping my posture.

I quietly opened the door to James' room and went to his bedside. He had one leg out from under the covers and his head against the wall. The blankets and pillows were a heap of destruction. I smiled and gently kissed his head, his light snoring only hesitating the briefest moment at my touch.

Back in the living room, I grabbed my bag and went to the kitchen to give Mary a kiss goodbye. To my surprise, she wrapped her arms around me and hugged me desperately.

"Be careful," she whispered.

I wanted to make a joke, but had the good sense not to. Besides, there was a tear going down her cheek and I didn't know if I could reply without breaking down myself. So, I went out to the truck.

The scenario replayed in my head as I sat at the boarding gate after going through security. It seemed silly. Ridiculous. I wasn't in any danger. Not physically. I decided the tear wasn't for my physical well being as much as it was with the discomfort that this trip, this whole Jesus encounter, had put on our marriage.

You will have to choose your life or what I ask.

Those words echoed in my head as I boarded the plane.

13

"Good morning, America. This is Samantha Gilroy. Today we speak with California pastor Bob Jordan. You've no doubt seen his face on the TV or your phone in recent weeks as he foiled a robbery and then was on stage at a Lucifer concert." Samantha's head cocks to the side as she speaks to the camera. Her face carries a what's-that-all-about expression.

"And he claims he did these things because Jesus Christ came into his office and told him to. That's coming right up after weather and your local news."

With that, the studio becomes a bustle of activity, reminding me of an ant farm I had as a kid. My babysitter for the day is a thirty something year old guy with blonde hair that has guided me throughout my preparation for the morning. His name is William and he's sharply dressed and wearing two rubber bracelets that look out of place and childish with his coat and tie. One is the neon green I continue to see more often, even in New York. The other is a rainbow. He has offered me food and beverage, made sure my clothing was presentable, and taken me to makeup so that the viewing public will be able to tolerate my face. The only thing that William hasn't done, although he has tried, is settle my nerves. My hands shake. I feel like I did when I went onto the "platform" at the concert two weeks ago.

William leads me on set where I take a seat on a plush comforter type chair. Samantha Gilroy sits next to me.

A technician of some sort adjusts a microphone above where I'm sitting as another lady touches up my makeup. They back off the set as the lights come back on to full brightness and the director counts down on his fingers until we're on the air.

I look for the camera with the little light on above it so I know where to look. Samantha welcomes back America, reading from a teleprompter and introduces my story. A screen behind the crew lights up with what I assume the nation is seeing. It is clips and soundbites from the internet as well as the footage taken by the Fresno affiliate during the week.

When the shaky footage of the Lucifer concert plays, I feel my stomach churn. The images are of me being laughed at and dodging flying cups of beer. None of what I actually said while on stage, however, makes it into the intro.

I force my hands to release their death grip on the armrest and I yearn for that feeling of the Spirit again.

Samantha turns to me with a couple sheets of notes in her hand and a very pleasant smile. She has incredibly white teeth. No more teleprompter. She'll be working from the notes and the interview will be more impromptu, seeing where the questioning takes us. Everyone has been very friendly, yet I am still uneasy.

"Pastor Bob, welcome to New York." The director has decided beforehand that Samantha will refer to me as Pastor Bob. I'm to call her Samantha. No Mrs. Gilroy.

"Thank you, Samantha."

She crosses her legs and leans towards me, her folded hands resting on a knee. I try to keep my hands still and not look like an idiot.

"Pastor, you've been quite a sensation lately, and I know everyone is incredibly excited to hear about your visits from Jesus."

Which I totally expected. It is all everyone is really interested in. So, I've come up with some answers of my own to try to get the conversation on track. "Yes, I know that seems exciting Samantha, but it was just a method He used to get me to share His love and forgiveness with the world. That's what I'd really like to…"

"Bob," she interrupts, already foregoing the pastor part, "can you tell us what he looked like?"

The interruption takes me aback just a little, but I'm determined to keep going. "In fact, if you were to play the concert tape in its entirety, you would hear me saying…"

"What did he look like?"

The second interruption makes my brain falter again. The lights. The bustle. I catch myself answering her question. "I don't know—like a guy, I suppose."

"Did he wear robes and sandals? How about the hair?"

"What?" I stammer. "No, he had on jeans. And His hair was short. Had a goatee."

Samantha gives off a laugh, and I think I hear a couple chuckles from the crew. "Pastor Bob, that's not what Jesus looks like."

In hindsight, I should have played along and answered the questions. Instead, I tried to get smart. Maybe a little snippy. Okay, definitely a little snippy. Things may have gone different if I'd played along. Unfortunately, I had to open my mouth.

"I'm sorry, Samantha, I didn't realize you'd met the man before."

Her smile went down. It didn't go away. She was too professional for that, but it did diminish. Just a tick.

There was a second of dead air before she recovered, the smile beaming back into place. But the eyes? The eyes made me sink deeper into the soft chair.

"Pastor, let's get to your message, shall we?"

I was wrong. Obviously, she could see I wouldn't be a pushover. What I didn't realize was that Samantha Gilroy wasn't here because she was just a pretty face. I didn't fully appreciate that a person didn't get to host one of the top-rated morning shows in the country without paying their dues as a journalist and reporter. Asking hard questions and laying traps, if that's what it took.

"Yes, thank you," I started, thinking I could now share the gospel with the country.

Wrong. Samantha charged in. "Your message, Pastor, seems to be that we all need Jesus in our lives. That He was sent by God. Why do we need Him?"

I could work with this. "Well, the big reason is because of sin in our lives."

I was confused, because I thought she was actually leading me down the path to sharing the gospel, but she looked like an angler who'd just set the hook. "So, Pastor, are we all sinners? Are we all evil and need saving?"

"Well, actually, yes. The Bible is clear on that. It says…"

"Is a two-thousand-year-old book really where we should be getting our living advice from, Pastor Bob?"

"Yes, Samantha, it's part of the reason God has left us His word. To guide us and to…"

"Yes, Bob, but some of these 'sins' are things like homosexuality and premarital sex and abortion…"

It was my turn to interrupt. "A lot of things we feel are commonplace separate us from our creator. The ones you listed seem to be the hot button topics, but adultery and lying are…"

"Please, pastor, don't you think society has evolved past the point of needing some ancient text to dictate right and wrong? How can we all be full of evil?"

I forced myself to calm down and not interrupt. I didn't need people tuning out as the two of us argued. But I didn't have to answer her question. "Samantha, it is not my job to force these ideals on you or anyone. I am just trying to…"

"Pastor Bob, the Christian community has a history of trying to force their idea of morality down people's throats."

She was on a roll and ready for a fight. I had to try and go ahead with what I came here to do. "But despite our sinful nature, our God, our Creator, loved us so much that He…"

"Pastor Bob, how do you respond to the accusations that your Jesus sightings are simply a ploy to fill seats and build your church?"

Her sudden turn in the conversation stopped me again. Her tactics were evidently meant to throw me off. Maybe they taught that in journalism school. It was working.

I stumbled a bit before muttering, "That is absolutely not true."

She referenced her notes. "I have been informed that giving to your church has quadrupled in the last two weeks."

"I never asked anyone for money."

She flipped to another page of her notes. The screen behind her showed the viewers a piece of paper that looked like an invoice or order form of some sort. I couldn't make out the figures or the logo. But there were lots of dollar signs.

"Pastor Bob, can you explain all of these bracelets that have been going around selling for five dollars apiece? Good Morning America has found the manufacturing plant that they come from in China and I find it repulsive that a Christian organization would profit from oppressed people under these conditions."

I was standing. I didn't yell, but my voice was not meek. "Mrs. Gilroy, I don't know anything about those bracelets. And we are not a Christian organization, we are the body of Christ. We believe that the Bible is the Word of God and that what it says is truth. That God created them man and woman. That the covenant of marriage is sacred. That there are things in this world that are contrary to a holy God and He cannot tolerate them."

I looked at the camera directly now. My voice softened, but it was still strong. "And yes, the church is full of sinners just like the rest of the world. We all fall short of the glory of God. But thank God that He loves us enough to send a way back to Him. That's the good news. That's the—"

Right then music started. But it wasn't angelic beings heralding the return of Christ. It was the commercial break cue. Samantha Gilroy had been staring at me, clutching her notes in both her hands. But with the music her demeanor totally changed back into the smiling hostess. "Thank you so much, Pastor Bob. When we come back, we'll be having an in-studio cooking demonstration with renowned chef Maria Shill with some spring time fare."

The commercial music rolled louder and we went into the break. My handler came to fetch me.

Samantha Gilroy patted my hand. "Sorry about getting rough, Bob. But it was a great segment. Thanks for coming on." And then she was off to get ready for the next part of the show. Like it hadn't affected her life at all.

I was shuttled off set to looks of distaste and disdain. William was very curt with me. As he saw me out the studio door, I was going to thank him for keeping me on track, but he left me with some words of his own.

"You know, my boyfriend's parents are Bible thumpers like you. They won't have anything to do with us. It's very difficult for him." He tore off the bright green bracelet and threw it on the ground.

I was about to say that I was sorry for his boyfriend's situation and to try to explain that I didn't believe the parents were handling things appropriately or in a very Christ-like manner, but I didn't get to. The door slammed in my face.

14

I hoped the interview was the end of the nightmare. That the humiliation would end there and I could just return home with my tail between my legs. You can't go on national television and have an argument with a person trained in debate, arguably come out on the losing side, and feel just hunky-dory afterwards.

But as I stepped out onto that New York City sidewalk, I didn't feel bad. Maybe a little beaten. Maybe not great. But not horrible. The horns and people and bustle. In the middle of downtown there was a giant TV screen on the side of a skyscraper and it was airing Good Morning America. Five minutes ago I had been up there talking about Jesus. I had gotten in the last word and I was getting used to Jesus's promises of these things happening. They were almost like signs that I was in fact doing what he had sent me to do.

Either that, or I was trying to justify to myself that I had flown across the country to preach the gospel, to evangelize to an entire nation, and I had to cram it into a ten second burst of oration. I hadn't even gotten the entire message out. Mostly I had just argued.

A cab pulled over and I asked the driver to take me to my hotel.

"Sure, bud, no problem," he said and started the meter.

His voice and accent were quintessential New York. His look was, too. Big guy. Old coat on, beret on his head. If he would have been smoking a cheap cigar, the image would have been complete. Like I was watching a movie.

Evidently, I looked at him a little too long and he went full New Yorker on me. "Hey, pal. You got a problem? You like starin' at me?"

I held my hands up. "Hey, buddy, I'm sorry. I didn't mean anything. You just kind of look familiar. Like a cab driver out of a movie." I smiled, trying to ease the sudden tension.

"You judgin' me, pal? You're that preacher that was just on the TV, right? Talkin' about how I'm the bad guy. I'm the sinner."

"I was never able to fully articulate what I wanted to say in there," I replied. "They didn't let me finish. What I was trying to say is that we are all, all of us, sinners. And that sin in our lives separates us from God."

We took a hard right-hand turn and centrifugal force pushed me against my door. Must be standard procedure. My driver didn't seem to mind a bit. "That's the problem with you Jesus nuts. Think you're better than everyone."

He pulled in front of my hotel and hit the meter. Looked back and said, " $14.75." I got out and handed him a twenty. He took off without offering me any change.

***

I grabbed another cab to the airport after getting my things and checking out of the hotel. I made sure not to stare at the driver but was surprised by how many people stared at me. And by the reactions I received. Some were encouraging, waving and yelling "God bless you, Pastor." Others were not so encouraging, ranging from dirty looks to middle fingers emphatically thrust my direction.

After checking in, I found a chair to wait for the boarding call. A young guy came over and sat next to me. He wore a neon green bracelet, but I didn't say anything. He recognized me soon enough, though, and we began to talk.

Real nice guy. His name was Bill. He was twenty-four and he'd been following my escapades online. Kind of weird to have joyful stalkers like that. He was nervous about his upcoming flight to Colorado to meet his sister. It turns out Bill's dad had had a daughter before Bill came along that no one knew about. All these years later, the sister actually had traced down her lineage and it had come to Bill.

"Well, that's kind of neat," I said. "Is your dad excited?"

Bill looked down at his feet. "Well, pastor, my dad died a couple years ago."

Oops. I didn't feel too bad, though. As a pastor, asking people about their personal life, you got used to sticking your foot in your mouth. "That's too bad. Sorry, Bill."

"It's okay. But anyway, I just worry that Julia, that's my sister, will hate my dad for not being around. That she'll hate me."

I leaned over, resting my arms on my thighs, and looked over at Bill. What could I do but try to be encouraging? He was a young man and had been when he'd lost his father. Then to find out that your dad had a secret life early on. Had made some mistakes by most accounts. But Bill also had this rare opportunity for healing and relationship.

That's what I wanted to show. That even though things may be seen as wrong or bad or whatever, that our God still uses those things for good. For His will. I'd seen it so often that it was hard to ignore. Sure, I couldn't see His purpose in all bad things, but I certainly didn't doubt His ability to use them as such.

That's what I wanted to convey to Bill. That's what I wanted to say and would have said. But we got interrupted. The day had been full of interruptions.

"Hey, you that pastor from Good Morning America this morning?" It came from behind us. I swiveled around in my chair to look at where the question had come from. From the tone, it didn't sound like cheerful recognition.

"Yeah," I said. "That's me."

This guy was older than Bill, but probably younger than me. He had on a black coat and boots that clomped, even on the carpet, as he came around the benches and chairs to where Bill and I were sitting.

He looked down at me with disgust. "Yeah, you're that guy alright." Like I had lied to him about being "that guy."

I'd had enough confrontations for one day. I also thought I could help comfort Bill. So, I said to this new guy, "Hey, pal, I was talking to my friend here if you don't mind."

But he didn't back down or even back up. He hooked his thumbs under the straps of the backpack he was wearing and said, "Oh, I bet. Telling him the same crap you were spewing this morning?"

How do you even respond to that? I mean, are you really going to win an argument with, or change the mind of, someone who disagrees with you so vehemently that they're willing to accost you in the middle of the airport? So, I turned my shoulders to face Bill, putting the new guy out of view. Kind of. Maybe if I ignored him, he'd go away. Bill's face was pointing at me, but his eyes were looking over my shoulder, uncomfortable. I felt crowded.

I stood up. "C'mon, Bill, I'll buy you a cup of coffee while we wait." I looked towards the Starbucks down the enormous hallway within the boarding area.

But the new guy didn't want to be ignored. He stepped into my face, between me and Bill. "How can you Christian freaks keep on and on about that garbage, man? That you can tell me how to live? Get real."

I felt more than saw that people had gathered around the little scene I was a part of. Phones were out. There was always someone filming nowadays. But New York or not, an airport or not, this was not the first time I'd been confronted by someone who didn't believe what I did. It wasn't the first time someone had been rude to my face. And I wasn't even upset or angry. The world would react this way.

"Hey, man," I started calmly, but not demurely, "I don't want to argue. They invited me on the TV show to share my view. That's all I did."

The new guy, however, did not need my permission to rant. His voice louder, he said, "My dad left me when I was five and I had to grow up on my own in this town. How is there God in that? Where was your Jesus? And my girlfriend got pregnant and now she left and I have to go to court all the time and fight to see my own child. Where is God in that? This fairy-tale crap you spew out there is just so stupid."

I did feel bad for the guy. He was hurting, too. But he was blaming my God for things that were not in His nature and, in a way, were not of His doing.

But I still didn't want to get dragged into this. "I'm sorry you're going through all of that," I said and tried to step around him.

He maneuvered into my path. Like a moving screen. His finger was in my chest now. "People don't need to hear your bull, man."

It was probably the finger in my chest.

"Look, how is it God's fault? When are we going to take accountability for the things we do? Your dad left you, God didn't take him away. God didn't tell you to knock up your girlfriend, you did that all on your own. I mean, how can we live a life doing the things God tells us not to do, in this two-thousand-year-old book, and then wonder why we have pain in our lives."

It came out louder than I'd wanted. Harsher. I had let myself get dragged into an argument. Again.

The guy's eyes showed a brief glimpse of understanding and maybe, just maybe, a hint of sorrow. But the anger pushed it aside. I thought he might hit me.

Commotion and argument erupted from the crowd. I resolved myself to keep my mouth shut and somehow slipped out of the increasing shouts and hollers. As I melted away, I saw a security guard heading that way and the people soon dissipated. Just like junior high. The guy with boots and the black jacket made his way down to another boarding gate. I looked around for Bill, but couldn't find him.

When they started the boarding for my flight, I made a quick trip to the men's room so maybe I wouldn't have to go on the tiny plane restroom on the flight home. When I came out, I spotted Bill in the next boarding gate waiting for his own flight. I noticed he no longer wore the neon bracelet on his wrist.

PART THREE: SEED AMONG THORNS

15

The flight back was uneventful. And long. The good thing was that between the flights and the layovers I had ample time to work on my sermon for the next Sunday. I had sent Dave a text to see how Dr. Jay had done. I thought he'd call, but no. Just replied with: **It was fine.**

Fair enough. I had plenty to do. This next sermon would be about the third soil type: the seed that fell among thorns. This was the one that people tended to resonate with, the one they felt the biggest tug on the conscience. When the worries of the world choked the Word in our life. How could I push our church to avoid this? To cultivate our soil?

There were lots of examples of thorns, but I had lots of ways to combat them. To make our soil fertile. It was time to push. To not be passive in giving the message, but to send it out as a challenge. Are we taking this seriously or not?

While I liked all of these sentiments, and they naturally intrigued me, I found it hard to stay on point. Hopping plane to plane and trying to make notes in crowded seats, it seemed reasonable to lack focus. But that wasn't it. I kept thinking about this revival idea. The logistics. The little details.

Fine. I had the rest of the week to dial in the sermon. I knew pretty much what I wanted to say anyway. Why let the revival be a distraction? I would start working on it.

Certain items needed priority over others. If I was going to announce this on Sunday for the following Friday, I'd better find a location to actually have it. Was a Friday best? And a time, of course. It would be nice to have sign-up sheets out for Sunday as well. Set up, parking, things like that.

I Googled and called people around Lamont, trying to find a venue. Most had a certain number of attendees attached to permits which limited capacity and while I'd certainly be happy with a couple hundred, I didn't want to limit what God might have in mind.

Google's algorithm must have thought I was looking for real estate. Soon, homes and land for sale started popping up in my search feed. One picture had a large white barn far off in the distance. It reminded me of a big tent.

That could work. Totally old school, but very quaint and humble, too. An old time tent revival.

I hopped aboard my last plane for home and put my phone on Airplane Mode. In my seat I tapped my leg and drummed my fingers, unable to sit easy. Evening crept in and I could see clusters of lights thousands of feet below.

The last layover was in Vegas, so it was just a small little jump to home. It was also a small little plane. I don't know what causes turbulence, but there was plenty of it. The lady sitting next to me must have taken my leg tapping as a sign of nervousness from the rough ride. She told me it would be alright.

***

The balmy evening air hit me as I got out of the Ranger in front of our house. Far different than the east coast. Springtime in the Valley. I could smell the blooms in the still air. A season of life and growth. Seemed appropriate.

Mary had left the outside light on for me, but both she and James were in bed asleep. I wanted to wake Mary and tell her about the revival and all the thoughts and ideas I had for it. I wanted her input. I tried to make a little extra noise as I got undressed and crawled into bed and she stirred, but never awoke. Or if she did, she never let on.

My mind was still a jumble of thoughts fighting one another. It was two in the morning and it had been all I could do on the drive back from the airport to keep my eyes open, but now, as I lay in bed, staring blindly at my ceiling, sleep was elusive.

The music! I needed to make sure the worship team was on board. And Tyler who ran our soundboard... could he do this offsite?

He'd need power. I'd have to rent a generator. I'd have to —

Stop. I just needed to stop. Today had enough worries of its own. I vowed to let God handle things and set about to seriously get some sleep.

When Mary's alarm went off for her to go to work, I was on my phone, looking at tent rental places and checking their hours to see when they opened.

***

When I got back to the house after dropping James off at school, Dave was parked there. He had his boat behind his truck and was leaning over the side going through fishing poles and messes of line and lures.

"Hey, Dave. Glad you came by. You going fishing?"

He looked up, holding one hand aloft, a hook stuck in the thumb.

"You're half right, Bob. We're going fishing."

Was he crazy? He knew before I left that I was going to be absolutely swamped with trying to get things together for this revival. He knew I would need his help. We didn't have time to go fishing.

"I can't, Dave. I've got a ton to do. I want to talk to you about it, but I don't have time to go out on the reservoir."

Dave went back to organizing gear. With his head over the side he said, "No better place to talk than out on the water."

I put my hands up to my forehead. "I've just got so much to do. After this revival, maybe we'll have some time we can go out."

Satisfied that things were in order in the boat, Dave stood up and walked over to me. His thumb had a drop of blood on it, but, thankfully, no more hook. "Look, pastor. You and I need to talk. About your revival, but also Sunday's service. Did Mary tell you?"

I looked away, like something in the distance suddenly needed my intense examination. "Uh, no she didn't. We ... uh, haven't had any time to talk since I got home."

I could feel his eyes on me. "Yeah, we should talk about that, too."

Elders could be stubborn at times.

I tried one more tactic. "Listen, by the time we get out on the water, go fish, clean the fish, load back up. It's just not going to work. I have to pick James up at two-thirty."

He placed a hand on my shoulder. I turned back to look him in the eye. There was compassion there. But there was something else as well. Worry? Sadness?

"Bob, I need to talk to you about me and Elena, too."

A couple of birds sang in the little mulberry tree by the road and I heard a tractor making its way down Main Street.

"All right," I said. "Let me grab a sweater."

***

THORNS

Dave took us along Main Street north, headed towards Bakersfield. The same route I had started on when going to the concert. We passed through the other small communities that lay on the outskirts of the big city, separated from each other by farming fields. Either orchard trees in bloom or row crops starting on their annual pilgrimage. The sun came in the passenger side window and it looked to be a glorious day. Full of sunshine and promise. Certainly not a day to be cooped up in your office, doing the things you should be. No, it looked to be a day of fun and messing around. But Dave's demeanor suggested that our own day would be serious.

Lake Ming sat against the south side of the Kern River. It wasn't all that large, but it was easy to get to, easy to launch, and supposedly there were plenty of fish. I tended not to catch fish no matter where I was, but I did enjoy being out on the water.

Dave didn't seem quite ready to dive into whatever he wanted to talk about regarding himself and Elena, so I filled the empty air with my own concerns. I went on and on about the Big Tent Revival. Maybe first annual, I had said. I told him about how much we had to do, especially get a place nailed down to have the thing so I could announce it on Sunday.

Dave stoically kept his hands on the wheel and his eyes out the windshield. His only verbal responses were grunts and nods. I knew he was listening though, because the grunts and nods were all in the right spots.

I finally got tired of hearing my own voice so I, too, became quiet and we rode that way to the lake. We got the boat ready to launch and Dave expertly backed down. I started his boat and held it close to the dock while he parked, but gave over the controls once he got back. He slowly made his way to a cove that he liked as I made up a couple of poles. He told me which lures to attach, but I had to hold up a couple of different styles until he approved. I didn't know a spinner from a bait-caster personally. Maybe why I never caught anything.

After dropping the trolling motor and settling into the pivoting bucket seat, the tension noticeably left Dave's body. It reminded me of my office, in a way. The place that I went to relieve the stress of life and to seek my creator. Surrounded by books and comforted by being in that space was where I had encountered God most often. Or the wetlands. This was Dave's retreat, and I felt honored that he would share it with me.

It was not lost on me that when Dave told me about the monumental things in his life, it had been on the lake. It was here that he had recounted his trips to Africa where he had witnessed a faith that he found both elusive at times, and, sadly, hard to find on this continent. It was also on the water where he had first been able to tell me about losing a child. And at the same time, but in a different way, losing a wife. Could my own difficulties within my own marriage lately even compare to that?

We cast about a bit. Dave got a bite. I got hung up in the weeds lurking beneath the water's surface. Dave reeled in and helped me get unstuck.

I started with what I thought would be the easy one. "So, what happened on Sunday? You said Dr. Jay did fine."

Dave never interrupted his casting and reeling. "No, Dr. Jay was fine. But we had some visitors this weekend."

"Not more news crews?"

"No, they would have been fine. Nope, we had protesters. Can you believe that?"

I hung up again, but was able to work the lure loose on my own. The sun felt splendid on my exposed skin. "Protesters? What were they protesting?"

"I don't know for sure. I think your message mainly. They are like this mystic group out of the bay area. They think that each person has their own way into God's presence. Or something like that."

Dave reeled in and switched out to a different lure. It looked the same to me, but a different color. I stubbornly stayed with my current setup.

"Were they bad? I mean, violent or anything?"

"No, they were quite polite, thankfully."

I thought about this message of the soil that I had been trying to reinforce lately in my church. It saddened me that I was apprehensive with my next question. "How did we react?"

Dave was quiet a minute. "We acted scared."

"Hm," was all I could muster. Would I have rather have had my congregation get in their face? Run them off? I don't know. But I think I would have preferred it to "scared".

I stared off to the bank as the water lapped onto shore. Just small little waves made from other boats or a slight breeze. Their pattern was hypnotic and I found my thoughts wandering about my church and its soil and what that soil looked like in a field of "scared."

Dave gave a tight grunt and from the corner of my focus his rod tip jerked. "Got one," he said softly and reeled in, keeping tension on the line. I snapped out of my daze and reeled in swiftly, then grabbed the net. Dave finagled the bass up to the boat and I deftly scooped the prize up. It was one of my finer performances.

A nice little bass. Nothing to write home about, but more than I'd caught . . . ever. Dave got the hook out of the lip of the scaly creature and lowered it back over the side. The tail flipped back and forth rapidly and then it was gone into the depths of Lake Ming.

A touch of a satisfied smile creased his mouth, but not the usual reaction. It wasn't because of the size of the fish, either. Fishing was Dave's thing and it didn't matter how big the trophy was. I didn't re-cast. He just sat there with a far-off look.

"What's up, Dave? What's really digging at you?"

A heavy sigh, then he looked at me. "It's Elena. She saw you on the TV yesterday."

She may well have. Elena hadn't been to church in a long time. I'd only met her on the occasions when we went over for dinner or had them over at our house. Something I said must have caused some rift between the two of them. Since they had lost their child so many years ago, Dave had prayed and prayed for Elena. That her relationship with Christ would be mended. That her heart wouldn't be hard. I'd prayed for it, too.

"I'm sorry, Dave. But I don't think I said anything bad or wrong or anything like that. Did you see it?" I was careful with my tone. I didn't want to seem defensive. I didn't feel defensive. But I wouldn't insult Dave by pandering.

"No, it's not bad, really," he said as he turned and faced me. The sun reflecting off of the lake was brilliant but made him squint, even with the sunglasses on and his brow scrunched under the brim of his hat.

I was quiet, allowing him time to move at his own pace. "Actually, something you said gave her a spark or something. She said she was coming to church next Sunday."

I remained quiet. Mainly because I didn't know what to say. That was good. Church attendance certainly didn't automatically make your relationship with Christ or the Father miraculously blossom, but it was definitely a step in the right direction.

As gently as I could manage, I said, "I'm confused, Dave. Isn't that a good thing?"

"I want it to be, Bob. I want it to be. How long I've waited for her to find her way back. To see that spark in her eye again. To see the sadness wiped away. And then she sees you on the TV and somehow it brings her back."

"So, what if she had just heard me preach a sermon on some Sunday? Would that have made it okay? Does the revelation have to come from you?" My tone had slipped and I not only sounded defensive, but possibly a bit antagonizing. I immediately regretted it.

"I'm sorry, Dave," I got out.

He lightly lifted a hand. "No, it's fine, Bob. It's not your fault. But the part of the story where you meet Jesus, I think that is what really touched her. What if she asks you to see Jesus or something?"

I looked down at my feet in the bottom of the boat. "I don't think Elena will do that. That seems unlike her."

Dave put a hand on my knee and I lifted my eyes back up. "It was real, right?"

I suppose it was painful and a relief all at the same time. Painful because Dave was the one that I thought actually believed me. And he probably had at the beginning. I know he had. This thing with Elena had evidently shed some sort of cloud over things. Made him doubt.

I looked him straight in the eyes. "It happened, Dave. Just like I told it to you."

He tapped my leg a couple times and smiled. "Good. I need it to be real."

***

We were only able to stay on the lake a couple hours before we had to head in so that I could get James. On the way back to Lamont Dave asked about me and Mary and I said that things had been a little tense. That she was having a hard time believing the Jesus thing and thought that this revival was taking it too far.

He let the Mary thing go, maybe because of his own doubt, and started peppering me with questions about the revival. Fine with me. I needed someone to bounce all of these ideas off of. My excitement was contagious, because soon Dave was coming up with his own ideas about things and how we could make it happen. He knew a farmer that had a big generator we could use for power and his cousin ran a rental place over towards Taft. They would have a tent and chairs. Dave would make a call.

As we were coming into Lamont, I noticed a big white billboard type sign on the side of the road. It was placed along the fence line of a large, flat piece of land. Just land. It hadn't been farmed for anything this year. I couldn't remember the last time it had been farmed at all. No doubt at one time part of a larger tract, but divided and divided and now it butted up almost into town. The sign said it was 20 acres and it was for sale or lease.

"Pull over, Dave," I said and tapped his arm. Maybe too hard.

"Settle down. What's up?"

He followed my gaze to the sign and recognition lit up in his face. "Looks perfect," he said.

I punched the number into my cell phone.

16

The church wasn't as full as it had been the last time I'd stepped to the pulpit. My usuals were there and in their customary seats. George Liston was already looking at his watch. Matthew was still with his mother and father, but no hood up and no ear buds that I could perceive. A couple of new faces also looked up at me, always a nice thing. I spotted Elena sitting next to Dave and I stammered for a second when I saw her.

The worship music had been adequate. The vibe was definitely lower than it had been recently. Certainly toned down since three weeks ago. No news crews this week either. Also, no protesters. It was like we were back to normal. But I didn't want us to go back to normal.

In fact, the whole town seemed to be back to normal. No excitement or fervor. The same cars parked at the bar day after day. Cars from my church mingled with cars that did not frequent our parking lot. I was still seeing the neon bracelets, but not too many on people's wrists anymore. I had spotted them littering the streets and in waste baskets in town. I felt bad about the ones in the street, like I was somehow responsible for them.

The only excitement to come my way was via the trustees, and it wasn't the kind of excitement that I really wanted. They seemed put off by the events of the last couple weeks. Well, mainly just this last week. While they had been on board with the revival at our last meeting, the act of me bringing it to fruition was rattling their resolve.

The money was in the coffers to accommodate the expenses I had been attaching to the church debit card, but all of a sudden everyone had a better idea of where that money could be spent. I argued how could it be better spent than sharing the good news with our community. But that wasn't the real issue. No, as trustees they had to hear about the backlash from what I'd been doing. They had to answer the questions about the crazy pastor who'd seen Jesus. They had to deal with coworkers who took offense at what I had been saying.

The things that I'd been doing and saying so publicly was now a reflection on them. They were tied with me and the pressure was getting to them. They wanted me to tone it down and it was very hard for me to try and reason with them without getting worked up and animated. Maybe that was the wrong approach.

Placing my hands on either side of the pulpit, I lowered my head and took a couple breaths. I had asked God to speak through me, like I always did, but I couldn't get this out of my head. This would step on some toes. It was the opposite of tone it down.

I glanced skyward, raising my eyebrows.

Before I started into my sermon, and before I announced, officially, the revival plans, I gave it to them.

"Folks, what are we doing?"

I scanned the entire sanctuary, trying to make eye contact with everyone. The silence became uncomfortable, and I let it hang in the air. I let it get uncomfortable because it was about to get worse.

"Are we just playing church here?"

I scanned again, silently. People adjusted themselves in their seats. Eyes looked down. I heard someone cough.

"For just a couple of Sundays, we were on fire again. On fire for Jesus. We were proud of our church.

People's ears were perking up. This place was packed. And not just with believers. I have to say there were likely a lot of skeptics, too. People looking for hope or answers or comfort.

"But now it's like we're over it. Back to the grind. Just another day at the office. Back to a comfortable faith that we only have to deal with for an hour or two every week."

Calling out people, especially your congregation, was tricky business. You weren't doing it to make them feel bad or to single them out. But in a sense, you were trying to make them feel bad. What I was specifically trying to do was get them to do something. Anything.

That something would likely be a few leaving this church. The message was too upsetting. I was going to get emails about how I was being judgmental. That was a favorite of both believers and non-believers. "I thought it said not to judge others." To non-believers, I may explain how that is not exactly what the Bible teaches. To professing Christians, I'd tell them to read their Bible.

But I'd come this far. We were going to see what this church was made of. "This Friday, we are going to have a revival here in Lamont. A tent revival. You've heard of those, right? And we are going to invite anyone and everyone to come hear the word of God preached there."

More scanning the crowd. More silence. More fidgeting.

I pointed towards the general direction of Bakersfield. "It is going to happen on that field that's been for sale on the edge of town ever since I got here. We are going to have a big tent and lights and parking and hopefully a lot of people and we are going to worship our God and share Him with this community."

A subtle change almost imperceptibly started to take form in those seats in front of me. People started to perk up. Just a little bit at first. As I continued without my impromptu soliloquy, I found my congregation seeming to respond. They sat up a little straighter and their faces started to show some resolve.

I gestured again towards the edge of town. "I called the number on that sign and we have leased that ground for this weekend. We have a tent rented, we have chairs coming, the worship team is prepared to take their equipment out there.

"But this takes the whole body. Not parts. You have a part, too. You are His body, so we need to act like it. Spread the word. Find me or Dave or a trustee and find out how you can help make this happen."

I needed to get into the sermon. I also needed to chill out with my rhetoric. To ease everyone into what the Word of God had for us this morning. To let them know that I wasn't judging them so much as I was calling them to action.

"We live in the most fertile farming area of the world. But we need our own soil to be fertile. We need the seed to grow. We can only complain about the state of the world so much before we start to actually act like what we read in our Bibles is how it is supposed to be.

"I know your pastor has acted a bit crazy lately and you may have heard some backlash from the community or even those closest to you. Those are thorns in our soil and it is time to get rid of them. So, I'm not going to back down now, I'm not going to change my story. Instead, I'm going to be louder and keep my foot on the gas."

I got a couple amens here. I had the feeling of the Spirit filling me again. That sense of confidence and peace that come from doing what God wanted you to do.

"Let's keep going with what God has to say to us and look at the seed among thorns."

***

THORNS

Most of the week involved getting things situated for the tent revival. There was plenty to do. But I had help now. Well, a few extra people besides Dave. My talk on Sunday had sparked a couple of volunteers. It was the best encouragement I'd had so far on this whole ordeal.

Dave had a small tractor with a mower attachment that he towed over to the lease property to mow down the weeds. Like I said, the ground hadn't been farmed in a long time. Hadn't been touched, really, so there was a backlog of dried vegetation to go along with this season's growth. It was quite a mess. The landowner was more than happy to have us mow it for him.

The generator and the tent would be dropped off Thursday. The chairs, too. Technically, logistically, everything was dialed in. As long as everyone did what they said.

And we had to get the word out. Marketing, if you will. I did two phone interviews for radio spots in the Valley, more to get the word out than anything. My encounter with Jesus was the impetus for the questions, but I dodged and changed the subject like a seasoned politician, turning the conversation to the direction I wanted to go. I told about the revival, making sure to get in time and location. I also got in a bit of the good news.

The word did start to spread, and not just throughout Lamont. The church had been spreading the word and there was a fervor growing. My landowner was actually getting nervous and vaguely threatened that maybe this wasn't such a good idea. I reassured him that there wasn't much we could do to his land other than improve it.

"What if someone gets hurt?" he asked. "Or worse."

I hadn't thought about that. There would be a lot of people and vehicles. Things sometimes happened. I remembered the protestors from when I was gone. Maybe we would have protesters again, and maybe these ones wouldn't be as peaceful as the last group.

I finally reassured him by promising to have the church get a one week rider on our insurance to cover the liability of the event.

This led to a phone call with Bill Matthews, the church treasurer and Gwen, our secretary. I had to coordinate the two: Gwen to research what we needed to do with our insurance company and Bill to cut the check. They both seemed put off, but agreed to work on it.

Bill was the most hesitant. He told me that despite the uptick in giving, we were rapidly about to exceed our excess and would have to start digging into savings. He didn't care for the revival idea. He thought the money would be better spent elsewhere and he brought up that sentiment again. I reminded him that same reasoning was in the Bible somewhere. Some guy named Judas had said it. That quieted him down.

Each trustee had a concern or problem or issue with the idea going forward that I had to reassure them about. My politician mode was extending beyond the radio waves.

A call even came in from the Kern County Sheriff's department.

"Hi, Pastor Bob," a familiar voice said.

"Who is this?"

"Sorry, this is Sheriff McKinney. I was one of the responders at the liquor store hold up a couple weeks ago."

Was it only a couple of weeks ago that I had looked into the barrel of a gun stuffed in my face? "Hi, Sheriff. Do you have some sort of update on the investigation?"

"Uh, no. Nothing on that front, other that I still say you were extremely lucky. No, this is about your revival thing that is coming up on Friday." He sounded serious. Formal.

"Yes, we have a big event planned."

"Well, that's the thing, Pastor. It's reached a lot of ears. We're hearing things. I'd recommend that you call it off. Bako-M may come back."

I placed my hand to my forehead, trying to put my thoughts in order. "Sheriff, I don't know that I can do that. Are you telling me that I can't or that you don't think I should."

Quiet. I looked at the phone screen. Still connected.

"Well, there are some in the department that think we should shut it down. We could bring up permitting issues and zoning ordinances to facilitate some sort of legal action to stop your church from moving forward. We know you didn't get any permits from the county."

"Sheriff, with all due respect, this is Lamont. We're close to the big city over there, but we're not the big city. We have impromptu parades here and no one ever cared. I certainly don't think that we are going to allow worry over a gang in Bakersfield stop us from doing what I feel God is asking us to do. Not just what I feel, but what His word says: to preach the gospel."

He sighed into the phone. "Yeah, I thought you might say something like that. I mean, you didn't back down from a loaded gun. But I did want you to be aware of what is happening. I'm pulling for you Pastor Bob."

"You think you'll come out for the revival?"

He was quiet again, thinking. "Kind of. I'll be on shift and make sure we've got a couple units in the Lamont area on Saturday night."

I smiled, though he couldn't see me. "Thanks, Sheriff."

***

The tent was set up by Thursday afternoon. Dave and I and a couple others set up chairs. Someone from the church had brought out a flatbed trailer to set the worship team on and we got that into position. We staked out an area for parking. A dumpster was delivered and put into place.

It was a great day to be out, too. The weather was brilliant. I had a light sweat going from the manual work we were doing, but it felt good and right to be outside and building towards this goal. This mission. I felt the sun burning my neck and ears. A small breeze had popped up and my nose was running, but still a perfect day to be outdoors working. There were clouds to the west and a chance of a springtime shower tomorrow, but it was supposed to hold off until the revival was done.

Dave and I went to a little sandwich shop in town for a late lunch around three. I was starving and ordered some sort of Italian sandwich, chips, and a soda. Dave got pretty much the same, and we took a seat at a small table out on the sidewalk.

I felt great. Between bites, I asked Dave, "How is Elena doing? Did she enjoy church Sunday?"

Dave chewed a little then swallowed before answering. "I think she's happy to be going again. To be coming back to her faith in Christ. I really want to ask her a lot more questions, but I don't want to push her too much either."

Sounded like a sound approach to things, so I just nodded.

"She wants to talk with you, Bob. She might be hung up with the meeting with Jesus deal. You good with that?"

"Sure. I can set something up if she likes. Or you can both come. Or lunch. Or whatever makes her feel comfortable. Whatever I can do."

"Thanks, Bob." He said it with genuine sincerity.

He opened his bag of chips and said, "And what about Mary? Is she still being hard on you?"

My chewing slowed. "I don't know. Things are strained a bit. I think she wants to support me, but she just has such a hard time believing some of the things I said about Jesus. She knows I experienced something, but she thinks it's more mental than spiritual."

"It's a little too much for a lot of folks. Maybe this revival will help."

I shook my head. "No, I do not think the revival is helping. It has kept me pretty busy. Frank Bowler called me at nine-thirty the other night. Mary wasn't happy about that either."

"Yikes. I'm sorry, pastor. But Frank can be aggravating no matter what is going on in our lives."

That got a chuckle out of me. Good ole Dave.

His mission accomplished, he stood up and said, "I'm going inside to use their restroom."

My head snapped up. "Crap," I said.

He gave me a strange look, "No . . . I just have to pee. Too much soda."

I stood up now, too, taking out my phone. "No, I mean, people are going to have to go to the bathroom. We don't have any toilets set up for that." I started Googling "portable toilets."

"Crap," Dave agreed.

17

The sun dipped just below the horizon as I pulled the Ranger into our driveway. There would be more setup tomorrow, but we had gotten a lot done. No doubt, there would be some hiccups, but the lion's share of the work was accomplished. And I had seven portable toilets scheduled for a noon delivery the next day. I guess the biggest hitch in the plans was that I didn't have anything to say. Between all of the coordinating and phone calls and site prep, I hadn't nailed down what I was going to talk about. Vague ideas floated in my head, but they needed to be fleshed out and prayed over.

My back was sore as I straightened up getting out of the truck. Someone had mowed their lawn close by and it seemed to put the exclamation point on an all-around good day. I went in the front door and heard the sounds of cooking from the kitchen. Despite the late lunch, my stomach growled at the smell.

I walked in the living room and James hopped up and gave me a hug while the TV blared in the background. He told me all about his day. How he and mom had gone to the park and he'd found all sorts of my bracelets in the trashcan but mom wouldn't let him bring any home. I reassured him that that was okay and went in to see Mary.

She stood at the sink scrubbing a potato and I put my arms around her from behind. It startled her and she jumped away, but not in a playful way.

I held my hands up. "Hey, Babe, didn't mean to spook you."

She shot me a look. Not a nice one, and said, "What are you doing, Bob?" She shielded her face and tried to shoo me away with a spatula. "And you are filthy. Go clean up."

Her tone was anything but pleasant, and she had not hidden her face in time. I saw the red rims of her eyes. The tiredness there. It broke my heart and my perfect day plummeted.

I took a step towards her. "Mary, what's going on?"

But she held a hand up. "Please, just go clean-up for dinner. It's almost done."

She turned back to the stove and started stirring something in a pan while I stood and stared, my hand still in the air. I wanted to say something or do something. Anything to ease her discomfort. But she had already shunned my touch and my words. I looked at the floor and, with no other recompense that I could think of, turned around and went to wash up.

***

Dinner was another quiet, somber affair. The clink of silverware against plates were the only sounds. Even James was quiet, moving his food around on his plate while looking at his mom and then me. I wanted desperately to say something. To ask about her day. To ask about what was wrong. But I saw no scenario where my words improved the situation. By divine intervention, I kept my mouth shut.

Sometimes we used to just sit on the couch and hold hands. No TV. No words. Just together. This silence was entirely different.

I cleared the table and did the dishes while Mary helped James get ready for bed. I set the dishwasher to start up in a couple of hours and went into James' room.

"Hey, buddy," I said and plopped down on his bed next to him, my feet hanging over the edge and my head next to his on the pillow.

He laughed and looked at me. "Dad, you're going to break my bed."

"I better go on a diet." He laughed some more. If only Mary was this easy to console.

James must have been tired, because he settled down pretty easy and nestled under his blankets and looked adoringly into my face. A lot of pressure for a guy who didn't even know why his wife was mad and had conversations with the Savior of the world.

"How is Tommy Chambers?" I asked.

James yawned and said, "Fine. We played dodgeball today."

I grunted happily. Another successful counseling session.

"Dad?"

"Yeah, buddy?"

"Is Mom sad?"

We try to hide things from our kids sometimes. Either we don't think they can handle it or they can't deal with it. But hiding anything from them is a false notion. Kids notice everything.

I sighed. "Yeah, I think she had a rough day."

"Why?"

I sat up and looked down at my son. I wish I knew how to answer his question. "I don't know, bud. Sometimes we have rough days. God gives us rough days sometimes."

It was a pretty big topic for a ten-year-old. I didn't know where to take it from here. But he left it alone and, instead, asked, "Are you going to make her feel better?"

I swear, that kid thought I was a miracle worker. "I'll do my best."

I stood at his door and turned out the light and looked back in. Sleepily, with his eyes closed, James said, "Maybe you should ask Jesus to help, Dad."

***

When I got in the room, Mary was in bed and reading her book. I quietly undressed and got in the shower and let the hot water soak away the day. The sweat and grime from a day spend outside swirled down the drain as the steam helped to relax my mind, cleansing my body and soul. I placed my hands on either side of the shower head and lowered my head below the stream of hot water and did what my son had told me to do: I asked Jesus to help make Mom feel better.

After toweling off I put on some sweats and a tee shirt. Mary had put the book down and turned off her reading light. She lay curled up, facing away from me. I was exhausted, but had planned on sneaking off to the extra bedroom to worry over my speech or sermon or whatever you wanted to call it that I was going to give tomorrow. I even made it all the way to our bedroom door when I looked back over at Mary laying there and I knew she was still awake.

I wasn't going to worry about tomorrow. Today had enough worries of its own.

I turned off the bathroom light and the bedroom was cast in darkness save a shaft of moonlight coming through a gap in our curtains. I gently sat on the edge of the bed on Mary's side, my hip touching her thigh. I began to rub her back. It was not sensual at all, I was just trying to comfort her in any way I could.

"Hey, Babe, we can't go to sleep like this," I said.

She was quiet for a minute. I started to think that maybe she had gone to sleep. But then she said, "I know."

The anger, most of it at least, seemed to be gone from her voice. But she still sounded tired.

I continued to rub her back. "I'm sorry I haven't been much help lately. Hopefully after tomorrow we can settle down a bit."

"Will it? Will it really settle down, or will Jesus send you off on another media campaign?"

Her anger was starting to kick back up, but she remained on the bed. She may have been crying again.

"I don't know, Babe. I just don't know. I'm trying to do what He asked me. Trying to do it the best that I know how."

"I know you're trying, Bob. And I want to be supportive, but . . . it's hard for me, you know. Harder than I thought it would be."

I didn't know why it was hard for her. Or I didn't want to admit why. Probably the same reason why it was hard for the trustees and a lot of people to get behind some of the things I was doing. Despite the miracle at the liquor store and being pulled onstage at some heavy metal concert, people just didn't believe the Jesus part. My own wife thought it was some delusion of mine.

I wondered how people would have reacted to these events if I had never mentioned having met Jesus. If I hadn't let slip that Jesus himself had given me a visit and told me to do these things, would they all be on the bandwagon? Or would they still doubt my motives and inspiration?

I sat there a long time in the dark and slowly continued rubbing her back. It helped me think and relax. It helped Mary relax, too. Maybe thirty minutes later, she did fall asleep. I leaned over and kissed her forehead and she sighed contentedly in her slumber.

I gingerly stood up and looked at the bedroom door. I hesitated. But I think I finally made the right move when I just got into bed myself.

18

As the sun went down that Friday evening, everything was perfect. The wind had settled down and the mid-seventies temperature was giving way to a very comfortable mid-sixties that should last well into the evening. The sunset was absolutely spectacular, painting the horizon in a vibrant orange which gave way to pink as the night edged closer.

Sound checks had been performed. The large tent had open sides and row upon row of empty folding chairs lay before me. Waiting for eager hearts to be set there. For their soil to be prepared and tilled and fertilized.

The generator was fired up and lights illuminated the parking areas and the inside of the tent. The rumble was audible, but nicely distant. I found I couldn't stand still and made my way to this item and that, checking and re-checking things. Volunteers from Lamont Community Church showed up to help with seating and to guide people into parking spots. I gathered them all up and we said a prayer to ask for guidance and for His Word to be heard tonight. I asked for the safety of everyone who came and I thanked God for a church willing to speak to its community.

Vehicles started to arrive with about thirty minutes to go until the scheduled start of the revival. At first, I was able to go and greet people as they arrived. It was a mix of young and old, white and brown. I would shake hands and thank them for coming. I prayed with some. Some were aloof.

Soon, there were just too many showing up to individually greet them all. The line of cars soon reminded me of that scene at the end of Field of Dreams when the cars are stacked bumper to bumper waiting to experience that magical field. The energy was electric and so far, everything was going off without a hitch.

News vans pulled in. Then a bus with a youth group from Fresno. I waved to people over the crowd when I recognized someone and would head over to say hello only to be sidetracked on the way there. I saw Dave and Elena milling about and they looked happy. As the time to start things grew near, I took my place on the stage. Towards the back, I saw Mary. She was going to stay as long as she could, but the babysitter for James had to leave at eight. I didn't know how long this was going to last, but I anticipated a late night.

The blur of people who had to stand stretched into the darkening landscape. All of the plastic chairs were filled. I could feel the butterflies in my stomach doing backflips.

I looked at my watch; time to go.

I nodded to our sound guy in the back and heard an echoey click as he turned my microphone on. I cleared my throat and gradually the talk and movement slowed down and soon all eyes were on me. I held a couple loose pages of notes in my hand and realized they were shaking.

I gave a brief hello and introduction then led the entire group in a prayer. At the end I was grateful for a thunderous "amen." With that, the worship team started out with one of our favorite songs from the church and the revival was underway. I stood off to the side of the stage and sang along, belting out the words. Hands were raised everywhere and, man, did it sound good.

At the end, the applause was raucous, with whistles and clapping and shouts. We went into another song and the energy stayed pegged. In some ways, it was remarkably similar to the Lucifer concert, but it was so much more. And it was pointed in the right direction.

The band went through four songs of worship music before I climbed onstage. My nerves kicked back in again. I would have liked to have been a little bit better prepared. I'd gotten up early to work on my message for the evening. It didn't need to be a sermon so much. What I needed was something simpler. Yes, this was to be a lesson from God's Word, but I had to account for those unbelievers and skeptics in the crowd. I needed to deliver Christ's message of hope to a lost people, but in its simplest terms.

I took my scripture for the evening from Paul's letter to Titus. I read,

> *"At one time we too were foolish, disobedient, deceived and enslaved by all kinds of passions and pleasures. We lived in malice and envy, being hated and hating one another. But when the kindness and love of God our Savior appeared, he saved us, not because of righteous things we had done, but because of his mercy. He saved us through the washing and rebirth and renewal by the Holy Spirit, whom he poured out on us generously through Jesus Christ our Savior, so that, having been justified by his grace, we might become heirs having the hope of eternal life."*

More amens emanated from the crowd when I looked up. There were some tears out there. A couple of swoonings. The lights from the TV cameras were bright, hiding most of the faces. I rolled up my notes and clamped them in my hand. I knew where I needed to go with this. What these folks needed to hear.

The plan was to break down this little section of scripture. I would start with how the world behaved now. How we behaved. And then I would move into how we had a loving God. A love we couldn't even fathom. How, even though our actions separated us from Him, He had provided a path back.

I had examples of how the world behaved. I had statistics and anecdotes. I would liberally sprinkle in moments of self-reflection. Opportunities to look within ourselves to see just where we sat with our Creator. More so, there would be plenty of moments for salvation. Invitations to grab onto what God had graciously offered us. To be with Him through the sacrifice of His son, Jesus Christ.

It was going to be awesome. Billy Graham stuff. Lives would be rescued for eternity. Our church would see what was possible. Our community would change and that change, fueled by love, would spread. Delusional? Perhaps, but my God was capable.

I drew a breath when a car with an incredibly loud engine flew by on the roadside. A muscle car, maybe. Quickly on its heels was a Sheriff's car, siren blaring and red and blue lights flashing, strobing about the tent roof. Heads turned to follow the cacophony of interruption as it receded in the distance.

I heard a nervous laugh come from my mouth. I wanted to say something clever, but couldn't bring anything to mind. I suppose Sheriff McKinny was trying to keep the riff-raff at bay.

I struggled to refocus. Closing my eyes, I frantically searched my feeble brain for indications of where I was at. Then the words settled in and I opened my eyes to start again.

That's when the second set of sirens started and another Sheriff's car, an SUV this time, roared by in pursuit of the first pair. Some people started to stand as everyone's attention began to drift.

As the noise cleared once again, I tried to restore a little calm to the crowd. "All right, folks. All right. Let's try this again."

But they wouldn't settle down. Heated conversations rose from the crowd. Bodies began moving and stirring. The worshipful excitement that had been so vibrant was giving way to a nervous energy. It felt dangerous, like a match close to a fuse.

I called again for a little order when a voice from somewhere in the middle said, "When are we going to see Jesus?"

This resulted in an instant uptick of talking and some shouts.

"Yeah, when does Jesus show up?" another yell came through loud and clear.

"Where's Jesus?"

Most people were on their feet now. A fight even started towards the back. I hopped off the stage, making my way there, thinking that it was roughly the same area I had seen Mary sit down. I was no longer passively asking for calm, but yelling my request into the microphone.

Sirens enveloped our gathering again as two more police cruisers blew past on the road. Things were falling into absolute pandemonium.

That's when the generator died.

***

We finally got the generator running again and the lights were back on, but it was too late. The same crowd which had rapidly gathered just as rapidly dispersed. In their wake were turned over chairs and trash all over the ground. Dust filled the air from all the vehicles pulling out of the farm field as angry horn blasts reverberated over the landscape, everyone trying to fight their way to the wire gate opening to leave the revival.

Revival. Not even close.

I hadn't seen Mary before she left. I texted her to make sure she was okay and she quickly responded that she was at home with James. That was a relief, at least. My sound crew was gone and all of the church volunteers had made their escape. I went and shut the generator off, noticing that one of the porta-potties had been pushed over on its side.

In the light of the moon, I picked my way back into the now desolate tent and sat in one of the plastic chairs in the back. My revival tent now looked like some deserted auditorium where the apocalypse had just run through.

I didn't know what I wanted to do. Cry? Yell? I was lost.

I heard light steps approaching and looked up to see a small figure coming my way. All I could make out in the light was a young man with a dark hoodie. My first thought was of the Bako-M gang and the warning from Sheriff McKinny and my encounter at the liquor store on Main Street. It seemed a fitting end to the evening.

But the mannerisms were not threatening and as the figure approached, I could see it was Matthew Liston. He no longer looked like the angry young man from a few weeks ago. Almost like he had compassion in his eyes. But it was dark, so who could be sure? At least he didn't have his ear buds in. Although, at this point, that may have been a relief.

He took an overturned chair and set it back upright, placing it next to me. We sat there in the dark.

"Heck of a show, Pastor Bob."

Somehow, I laughed. "Yeah."

He put his elbows on his knees and looked straight ahead. We both stared that direction.

"Did your folks come tonight?" I asked.

"Naw. Just me. They're coming to pick me up in a little bit."

Then, quieter, he said, "I liked where I think you were heading with your sermon tonight."

Weird. Here was this teenage kid that I probably thought was a lost cause and he was trying to comfort me.

"Yeah," I said again. "It was going to be good, I think."

His appearance here did have me puzzled. I turned and looked at him and said, "You know, Matthew, I really didn't expect to see you here tonight. This sort of thing doesn't seem like it would be your cup of tea."

He grinned and leaned back. Then he let out a sigh and said, "I know what you mean. Couple weeks ago, I wouldn't have been caught dead here."

"That so? Why the change of heart?"

"You know that concert you went to? The Lucifer concert?" He eyed me apprehensively. It's the look I get when someone who knows I'm a pastor lets out a swear word.

"Yeah, kind of hard to forget that one."

He smiled. "Well, I was there. I wasn't supposed to be. I told my folks I was going to Sam's house to study. Somehow, they bought it. But I went to the concert and something you said there really got to me. I couldn't shake it."

I was very intrigued, to say the least. "Really. What was it? You didn't throw anything at me, did you?"

He laughed, but then got serious. I felt bad about making a joke out of this moment. "Sorry, Matthew. Sometimes I use humor to deal with things."

He finally turned and looked at me. "It's okay, pastor. What you said was even though we were sinners, Christ still died for us. Something like that."

I looked into his eyes and saw no mocking. No hate. Just a yearning for explanation, for understanding.

I must have been quiet too long, because he said, "You did say that, right?"

My turn to laugh. "Well, kind of. I said it, but it is from the Bible. Not my words, really. It's from Romans. What struck you about it?"

He wiped his palms on his pants legs and let out a sigh. "I don't know. That I'm a sinner, I guess. That I've done bad things. Things I knew were wrong, but I did them anyway. Things I knew God didn't want me to do and I thought that He wouldn't like me because I did them. But even then, He still died for me. Jesus died for me."

With the faint light of the moon, I thought I could see moisture in his eyes. I found I was a little misty myself. Must be the dust. I decided not to bring it up.

Instead, I put a hand on his shoulder. "That is actually great, Matthew. People go their whole lives and never make that realization. It is God speaking to you, through His words. He reached to your heart. And He wants to forgive you. You have to ask Jesus into your life. Your heart."

I know I saw a tear fall to the ground, but again I let it go. He asked, "So, do we do some sort of prayer now?"

"I'd love to pray with you, but I'm not going to lead you in the sinner's prayer or anything like that. This is between you and God. Anything I say doesn't matter. It's what's inside you."

I did pray with Matthew then. I prayed with him and for him, never taking my hand off his shoulder.

When I was done, I clapped his back a couple of times and tried to lighten the mood. "So, going to be at church tomorrow?"

He raised his head and wiped at his eyes. "Are you kidding? I can't wait to see what you're going to do next."

That got us both laughing. A car pulled up to the edge of the road, its brake lights bright in the night.

He hopped up. "That's my folks."

He started to trot off, but stopped a couple steps away and turned back towards me. "Thanks, Pastor Bob."

I felt my grin bunching up beneath my eyes. I wanted to say, "No, thank you," but found I couldn't. Not if I didn't want to start crying full force. So, I gave him a wave and he went to the waiting car. I watched the taillights as they disappeared into Lamont proper.

PART FOUR: GOOD SOIL

19

The crickets and frogs were in full swing. A hint of moisture in the air dug into my bones as the excitement of the evening let down into a melancholy of sorts. All of a sudden, I was tired. Quite frankly, I was tired of the whole deal. A small piece of paper, maybe a gum wrapper, carried across the floor between overturned chairs, caught in some light breeze.

I stepped out of the darkness of the tent into the semidarkness of the outside, the only lighting from the mostly full moon high above. I looked at that moon, up in the heavens. Somewhere up there I'd always imagined God resided. Watching over us. Not exactly just watching. But kind of.

I stood there a good long while. My hands in my pockets. The goose flesh sticking up on my arms and the tiny breeze moving the hair on my forehead. I didn't plead or ask God anything. I was just there, looking up towards His supposed home, though I fully believed He was truly everywhere. I had been so sure that this was His will.

My phone vibrated in my back pocket. I pulled it out and saw a text from Mary.

You all right?

I sent back a thumbs up emoji and said I'd be home soon.

The ground which had been loose soil before this had started was now firm underfoot, trampled down by an onrush of people and vehicles. Now, just as suddenly, it was deserted. A flap from the tent started whipping behind me. The headlights of the Ranger had caught some of the moonlight as it sat waiting for me in the distance, its engine now cold as it sat alone.

Small twinkles danced in the moonlight amongst the earth underfoot. Discarded neon bracelets bearing witness to a now dark platform.

I didn't use the light from my phone. Instead, the dark accompanied me as I made my way back to the truck. I opened the door and got behind the wheel, staring ahead at the tent. A dead idea. Something that had seemed so full of potential. It was dark in the truck. My dome light had evidently gone out again. Or, with the way things had gone today, maybe my battery had drained.

I reached for the keys but they weren't in the ignition. I typically didn't lock the truck. Usually didn't even take the keys out. I rested my forehead on the steering wheel and thought about texting Mary again.

"Looking for these?"

That certainly woke me up. I about jumped out of my skin, ramming my body against the door, searching for the handle.

Then I recognized Him.

I suppose I should have bowed down or cried with reverent joy at the man in front of me, holding a set of keys in his hand. What slipped out of my mouth, however, was, "Oh, it's you."

The moon through the windshield cast deep shadows across his face. His eyes shined under those heavy brows. His teeth seemed very white in the dark. The smile still had a very calming effect. Not calming, exactly. Peaceful. It lifted a weight off of your soul. How could anyone be angry at such a smile, much less nail Him to a cross? But then I remembered some of the looks I'd received lately. I thought about the doubt I'd had when we'd first met.

"I'm sorry," I said, a bit sheepishly. "You took me by surprise."

His look never faltered as he put the key in the ignition for me. "It's alright, Bob. You've had a long day. Not all fun."

Somehow, I looked away from him and peered back through the windshield at the tent with one flap waving in the air. Many years ago, I had committed my life to this man. To this God. Theologically, I knew that He knew all about me. And my thoughts. And my worries. But I laid them bare before him regardless.

"You know, it has been a rough day. Highs and lows. And then highs again. The revival thing… I thought that's what you wanted me to do. And it was such a failure. But then Matthew at the end."

I let out a huge breath then turned back to him. "Was this about Matthew?"

He looked up at the roof, choosing his words. "Yes, I suppose it was. But it was about you. About you spreading my word. It was about all of the people that heard my word through you."

I was quiet, rolling what he said around in my head.

"The things I did, were they …" I didn't know how to ask it other than bluntly. "Did I do a good job?"

He laughed. "Bob, you did great. You did what your Father wanted."

"So, the revival was a good thing? And the interview?"

He turned in the seat to face me. "Look, Bob. Those may not have been the way I would have done things, but you spread my word to people who needed to hear it. You can't help how they take it. I mean, who goes to a concert by a band named Lucifer to preach my word? Classic."

He laughed even harder. Real comedian, that guy. I think that's why you don't see much joking around in the Bible. People just don't get his sense of humor.

I waited for him to go on, but he folded his hands in his lap as he looked at me. His eyes were very intense. He closed them for a second, then let out a sigh. I imagined his disciples heard this sound often when they weren't getting the point.

I wanted desperately to get the point.

Instead of any deep insight, he said, "So, how is the sermon series going? What did you call it? The parable of soil?"

"Soils. The parable of the soils. I can't believe you don't remember that one."

"I gave a lot of parables. Yes, the four soils. I remember. How do you think it's going?"

My turn to let out a deep breath again. "I don't know. This has all been crazy, but I don't know that the soil of the people in my church has done much. They're still laggard or disengaged. No matter what I say or advise I give. Our soil seems… unfruitful."

He put a hand on my shoulder, the laughter gone now. "Bob, I want you to read that parable again when you get home. Read it from how Matthew tells it. I think he says it best. There is something you are not seeing."

I didn't want to doubt what Jesus had just said to me. But I was preaching from Matthew's rendition of the parable. I had the thing memorized. I could practically recite it word for word. How was there something that I wasn't seeing?

His mention of going home caused a little bit of pause. Mary thought I'd gone off the deep end with my first Jesus encounter. Bringing up a second meeting wasn't likely to help.

He must have noticed a change in my demeanor. Or he was omniscient.

"I know things have been strained at home."

"Yeah," I said. "Things have been awkward and a little cold."

"Better than lukewarm, at least." He was smiling, but not laughing.

I forced a grin. "Well, I prefer them not cold. I know Mary believes in YOU, but she is having a hard time with me meeting you."

"I know, Bob. And I told you this would not be easy. Remember when I said you would have to choose your life or doing what I asked?"

"Yeah, the liquor store thing was very intense."

"That's not what I meant."

He looked serious again. I didn't like where this seemed to be heading. "Lord," I said, the word seeming strange, but it just came out. "I don't understand."

He smiled again, but not with humor this time. Only love. "I know. But I think you'll figure it out."

I guess that meant he wasn't going to spell it out for me. Looked like more cold at home.

"I have to go, Bob. And you need to get home. But before I go, I have one more message for you to share. Tell Dave and Elena that Gabriella is fine. They'll understand."

Which was good, because I had no idea what He was talking about. It was becoming a common theme.

He reached out and placed his hand on my arm. I looked Him in the eye. He said, "I have something to tell you about Mary as well."

***

Bugs had gathered around the porch light. I shooed them away with one hand and quickly entered the house. No smell of dinner this time. Mary had probably gotten a bite on the way home for herself and James. I went into the bedroom and heard the shower running, so I went to James's room and quietly opened the door.

He stirred when I came in, sleepily rolling over in my direction, his eyes only half open. He smiled when he saw it was me. What more could a father ask?

"Hi, Dad. How was your show?"

I sat on the edge of the bed and put a hand on his back. "Not the best show ever, but it will probably be the talk of the town."

"That's good," he said and his eyes closed again. I continued rubbing his back. *My show.* Even a ten-year-old knew what it was. A show. A spectacle.

But not all bad. Jesus didn't say He exactly gave it the green light, but He also didn't seem disappointed in it. He'd seemed pleased.

I gently got back up and went out the door into the hallway. I made my way through the house turning off lights and locking doors. The fridge held little in the way of a dinner, so I grabbed a bit of left over chicken from the other night and called it good.

Mary came out of our room in her pajamas, her hair up in a towel. She knew how the revival had gone and looked at me with pity. Like you would look at a dog who'd been left outside all night.

"Hey," she said.

"Hey," I came back.

I had taken a seat at our kitchen table. Just sitting in the dark eating a chicken thigh. She came over and sat as well. Her hands were set up on the table and after wiping my hands, I took hold of one of hers.

"Sorry I didn't get you any dinner," she said. "I thought you'd be later."

I didn't say anything, just squeezed her hand. It was nice. We hadn't had very much one on one time in the last three or four weeks. But I had so much to tell her about tonight.

"Babe, I think things are going to slow down a bit now. No more revivals. I don't think, at least."

She smiled again, but still with pity in her eyes. "That's good."

"No. Well... yes... I don't know. But please hear me out. As I'm sure you gathered before you left, the revival did not go well."

"It was a little wild, but I wasn't able to stay long. Sorry, Bob, but the sitter for James had to leave." She lowered her head, but looked up under her brow at me. "But it's been on Facebook. And the news. And everywhere."

"Yeah, I'm sure. But it doesn't matter. I saw Jesus again."

Her gaze dipped for just a moment. My wife, the most patient person I knew, was angry. I had half-way expected it, but it still hurt.

"Listen, Bob, I think we probably should have talked about this before, but this has to . . ."

"No, Mary, I need you to listen..."

She pulled her hand from mine and stood up. "No, Bob. You can't keep doing this. It seemed weird but okay because you were still going out and talking to people about Jesus, but it's gone too far. The TV interview, the revival thing. You need to focus or see someone about this."

"I'm not imagining it."

The pity was back again, but love had also overtaken her angry look. A passing car outside briefly flashed her face with light and I could still see the love there. And the concern.

"I think you are, Bob. Just like the liquor store. These traumatic events are triggering something in your head. It could be serious."

I stayed sitting, my demeanor calm. "Do you want to know what He said?"

She turned her head to the kitchen, like she was looking for help. She came back to me. "I don't know that it's healthy."

I patted the chair she had left. "Have a seat. Humor me just this once. And then I'll let it go or see a shrink or whatever you want."

She crossed her arms and looked at me doubtfully. But she finally relented and sat down. I took both of her hands in mine this time. I looked into her eyes.

"He told me you were going to leave me."

She started to pull her hands back, but I put on just enough pressure to keep them in mine. She rolled her eyes and said, "That's crazy. I would not leave you. You've been acting insane lately, but I wouldn't leave you."

"He wasn't talking about now or during this last month. He said before we were married, you were going to leave me. That I was being an ass, which, as I recall, I was. And you didn't think it was going to work. Back when I was in seminary and when you worked in that coffee shop. He said you were going to leave me."

I said all of these things, but I wanted her to know that I was okay with all of it. She had thought about leaving me. Fine. I could take that. I could even understand that. And I was okay that she hadn't told me. I mean, she hadn't left, so what was the big deal?

As I said those words, I could follow the emotions of change on her face. It was too dark to see her whole face, but her brow told the story. Anger to confusion to some sort of shock. When I got to the last part, the look turned to amazement.

"And He said you didn't leave because He told you not to."

She did take her hands away this time. One hand went to her mouth and I could see moisture in her eyes glinting in the meager light of our dining area. I couldn't read her look now. I didn't know if I should try to hug her or maybe run for my life.

Soon enough, she answered for me. She dropped down and wrapped her arms around me. She sobbed into my shoulder as I wrapped my arms around her shaking body. I held my wife as she wept.

Eventually, after her breathing had returned to normal, she leaned back. Her face held a smile. "I have never told anyone about that before. Not my mother, not my best friends, not a diary. Never."

"But you told Him."

She gave a small laugh. "Yes, I told Him. I asked Him over and over for guidance and I never heard anything. On that night that we went to that fancy Italian place, I was going to call things off. Give you the ring back. I prayed one more time, and He answered. He answered directly. A voice. It was amazing."

I was smiling too. I couldn't help it. "And He said don't leave?" I don't know why I asked that. I guess I just wanted her to keep going with the story. Of course He'd told her to stay.

But she shook her head. "No. He said, 'Give him time.'"

I had a pretty good laugh at that. And then Mary was laughing too. Soon we couldn't stop. She finally managed to say, "I'm still waiting."

I don't know how we never woke up James.

20

Most Saturdays were spent getting my sermon ready. Making sure everything was dialed in for Sunday service. Getting all of the pieces in place. Our church had a lot of little details that someone had to take care of, but I guess that's why I made the big bucks.

Mostly I made sure my sermon was where I wanted it. Often, I would say it out loud to see how things came out or to make sure I could pronounce some of the Bible names I would be encountering. Sometimes major revisions were the order of the day. While a sermon is, hopefully, God's message for His people coming through your mouth, it is still something that you, as a pastor, create. I found that the longer you spent with that sermon you came up with, the more you disliked it. At some point you felt that it was horrible and everyone else would think it was horrible, too. Or they'd decide you were a heretic or something like that.

Some Saturdays, you didn't have anything. Usually that was because you had put it off all week, but mostly it was because you were uninspired. Or you were going through a part of the Scripture and you couldn't find the applicable point to the passage you were dealing with. On those Saturdays you had little choice but to lock yourself in your office and come up with something, anything, to share with your congregation the next day.

You know, usually they were just fine. You'd spend all week worrying about it and it was fine.

Sometimes even good. Last minute or something you'd planned out months in advance and, mostly, it came across satisfactory. My opinion is that happens because you're dealing with God's Word and the Spirit does indeed guide what comes out of your mouth from the pulpit. Quite frankly, I can see no other reason I was able to pull it off week after week. Sure, sometimes you gave a real stinker, but, by and by, most of my sermons were just fine.

On this particular Saturday, however, I had nothing. No sermon. No clear direction. I wasn't locked in my office freaking out about it, though.   Nope. Instead, me and my family were at the park. It was gorgeous out, even with the surrounding trees in full bloom and I could feel the tickle of an itch at the edge of my eyes. The sun was brilliant. Even the shadows seemed to have a crisp and distinct edge.

It wouldn't be long before the heat of summer started. But today? Today was simply sublime.

James kicked a soccer ball with some of the boys from his school who had gathered. Mary and I sat at the picnic table under a mulberry tree, listening to the young boys play. We both had our Bibles. I also had a notebook. There were a lot of things crossed out in that notebook.

"You sure He said Matthew?" Mary asked.

Without looking up, I said, "Definitely. He said Matthew captured the essence of what He was saying the best."

I started to reread Matthew's version. Again. For like the thousandth time. I heard pages flip in Mary's Bible, then she said, "All of the accounts are remarkably similar."

"I know," I said. "But evidently something is a little different."

I closed the book and looked up. The boys were laughing and running and kicking and falling on the ground. I couldn't help but smile. Any other Saturday when I didn't have a sermon, I would not be this calm or at peace. But today? I don't know, but everything was good. Maybe I just figured God would give me something. He always did.

"I wonder why the heading is 'The Parable of the Soils'?" Mary asked.

"Hmm?" I mumbled, turning my head towards her as she brought me back from staring off into space.

"Well, I saw the heading in your Bible and it's the same in mine. 'The Parable of the Soils.' But Jesus doesn't call it that. Look at verse 18. What does He call it?"

I flipped open my Bible again. Putting my finger on the page, I went to verse 18 and read, "'Listen to what the parable of the sower means.'"

The sower, I said in my head again. Maybe that's why Jesus hadn't seemed to recognize it. He referred to it as the parable of the sower, not the soils. Potato, pah-tah-toe.

The soccer ball came close to our table and I hopped up and kicked it back to the boys.

***

Around lunch time, Mary and I sat on the same side of the picnic table and watched the boys. I held her hand and gave a little prayer of thanks. Thanks for this woman and thanks that we had made it through the little rough patch that my Jesus encounter had rendered. The rough patch that had both strained and strengthened our marriage.

The boys were slowing down now. Instead of the full on soccer match, they were taking turns as goalie and penalty kicker. Of course, being boys, there was a lot of falling and laughing. I may have been a little jealous.

Two of them picked up the ball and headed off across the park. James gave a wave and then trotted over to where his mom and I sat.

"Hey, Buddy, the game finally over?"

"Yeah, Tommy and his brother had to go home for lunch."

I assumed that was the infamous Tommy Chambers. On cue, my stomach growled.

Mary looked over. "Sounds like Dad's ready for lunch, too."

We started to gather up our things when I got a call from Dave. He wanted to go to lunch. Everyone was hungry, it seemed. I started to tell him that I was hanging out with Mary and James, but if it was real important we could figure something out. But he was hoping that all of us could meet not only him, but Elena too, for a bite to eat.

The place he wanted to meet was a small taco stand that set up just out of town off the main road. They were called a "roach-coach" when I was a kid. Now they were food trucks. I knew the place and the vendor. It made my stomach growl again.

I hadn't spoken with Dave since the revival. We were going to head there this afternoon to clean up with some other folks from the church. Frankly, I hadn't wanted to talk about the revival much at all. I did want to talk about Jesus again, but it was a hard subject to broach. I didn't know if I wanted to tell anyone about it considering the backlash the first one had caused. Then again, maybe that was the point.

I pulled onto the shoulder next to the farm field where the roadside stand was set up. A couple of cars were already there. A group sat on a blanket at the edge of the farm field, eating tacos. We grabbed an empty picnic table.

This field was in contrast to the one we had the revival in. It was planted with something. Crop identification wasn't my strong suit, especially at this early stage of development. But the row of short bright green seedlings stretched so far that you couldn't really decipher the end of the field. It appeared to stretch on forever until the foothills poked up out of the ground on the distant horizon.

Dave's white Dodge pulled up and parked next to our car. We exchanged welcomes and hugs. It had been some time since I had seen Elena other than out in the crowd recently. She looked good. Happy. I didn't know if I should shake her hand or give her a hug. There was a strange vibe with her reassessing her faith because of my Jesus encounter and Dave's unease over that whole dynamic.

But good roadside Mexican food tends to smooth out all sorts of things. I think that's in Proverbs somewhere. It wasn't long before we were all at the picnic table reminiscing like good friends. James was polite and answered questions thrown his way about school and church and sports.

Occasionally a car would speed down the road past us. The faint hint of exhaust would hit, but the smell of the taco truck would overpower it again. The sun was as brilliant as it had been the day before when we had set up for the revival. My neck was extra warm today, indicative of the sunburn I had evidently procured yesterday.

Dave and James went and got our food when it was ready and brought it back to the table. We sat around and Dave said grace. We even all held hands and when we said "amen" at the end, it seemed that Elena said it louder than the rest of us.

It was just plain old good. No pressures of revivals or TV shows. Just catching up and ribbing each other and good food. A time or two my sermon tried to invade my thoughts, but I pushed it back, doing my best to enjoy this bit of time God had allowed.

James, as usual, plowed through his food. Soon he fidgeted as his ten-year-old energy had not been hampered by his soccer escapades of earlier in the morning. The talk of grownups was not his idea of a good time. I told him he could go play by the edge of the field, but made it clear not to disrupt or step on the crops planted there.

Playing on field edges was fine sport for a young boy and James took off to look for bugs or lizards or any other trophy he could come across. Elena seemed to look that way often and I thought maybe she was worried about the boy getting into some sort of trouble or mischief.

"It's okay," I said to her. "He'll stay in sight and won't go near the highway or get in the crops."

She looked at me quizzically and then my comment registered. Smiling, she said, "Oh, no, it's not that. I was just looking at the field. You know, I grew up on that field."

I knew the short version of Elena's early life. That her family had lived on a farm somewhere close to Bakersfield before the property got sold to a large farming conglomerate. When that had happened, her family had to leave the farm and moved into Bakersfield itself. Her Father died, her brothers got into trouble, and Elena had troubles of her own. Through her mother, she had found Lamont Community Church, and she found healing there.

That was before my time as pastor. She and Dave had met at the church and grown up as a married couple there. They had become pregnant and seemed the idyllic American family. Until the baby died during the delivery. That is when Elena's faith had... what would you call it? Left? Took a hiatus? It was a theological question that I didn't want to delve into at the moment. But her and Dave's opinion on God and Christ and faith had diverged then.

THORNS

Most of my information I got from Dave. I know he struggled with his wife's faith and the strain the lost child had put on their relationship. Not that it was always mean or bad, but there was always a separation there. They had lost something precious to them and Dave continued to see God as wise and good. Elena had a hard time sharing that point of view.

But I didn't know that the farm where she had grown up had been right here in Lamont. "You grew up in this field here?" I asked.

A car went by and the wind from its passing kicked up the hair on her forehead as she continued to gaze out over the expanse of the farm field. "Yes."

We all looked at her now. She continued her story without much emotion. Like she was recounting raw facts. Quietly and calmly, she said, "You can't see it now, but there used to be a big oak tree about a hundred yards in. The driveway was off the little side road back there and it led over to the oak tree and the little house we lived in. A little yellow house with three rooms."

Her voice started now to carry some emotion. Happy reminisces. She smiled while her eyes remained on the field. "I was the only girl, so I got my own room and the boys had to share. But it didn't matter, because we never stayed in the house that much. We played out in that tree or out in the field. Hardly ever wearing shoes. The soil on our feet and our hands. Going with my father for farm chores."

She got up, almost in a trance, and walked towards the field's edge. Dave followed. Mary raised her eyebrows at me. I shrugged and we both got up to follow as well.

We were all quiet for a beat. Elena squatted down and picked up a handful of the dry soil, running her thumb through it. "Sometimes I like to look at that field right after it's been plowed. To look at the soil unearthed. It reminds me of the people who were there at one time.

The ones who planted the field. I wonder if these men who work the fields now have the same love of the soil."

I just couldn't escape soil these days.

***

We found our way back to the table. I had one more thing to bring up while Elena and Dave were here. Best that Mary was here, too. It was weird and strange and difficult to bring up. Not something that had a nice casual segue.

"Hey, Elena, before we go, there is something I'd like to talk about."

Dave eyed me. Like he was wondering why I would interrupt what had, to this point, been a great day.

I put my hands in my pants pockets. My shoulders drooped. Elena looked at me, a smile still on her face.

"Well, you see, Dave says that you've been going back to the church. And I think that is fabulous. It's great. But he says that one of the reasons may be because of my encounter with –" I paused and looked around before continuing with the big secret. "With Jesus," I finished.

She beamed. "Yes, it was a wonderful story. A wonderful experience, Bob. It has rekindled something in me. Thank you so much. It must be very awkward to try and share something like that."

I saw a couple of doves shoot by overhead. "It is wild, to say the least. I kind of wish that I had kept it to myself. Not because I want to hide it, but a lot of people have a hard time believing it. Totally fair, of course. It sounds like some crazy guy talking."

I made sure I never looked in Mary's direction. I tried to avoid all of their eyes, actually. But somehow Elena caught mine. They were clear and brown and they were asking me to go on.

I shuffled my feet. "Well, I just don't know if coming back to the faith or finding your faith again or however you want to put it…" Wow, this was weird. "I just don't know if that should happen because some guy says he saw Jesus. Does that make sense?"

She tipped her head to the side and scrunched her eyebrows. "But, you did see Him, right?"

I kicked a dirt clod. "Yeah, but it seems just not right. Like it is not the way to find it. Or maybe that it won't be a lasting experience."

She looked at me as if she were consoling a child. She put her hand on my arm and made sure I was looking into her eyes. "It wasn't so much your meeting with Jesus, Bob. It was something that I had forgot somehow. Something you said in your TV show that reminded me."

I could see her eyes get a little misty. "You said that God loved us so much that He sent a way for us to be with Him again. I don't know how I forgot that, Bob. I was so angry and shameful and I thought He didn't love me anymore. But your talk with that lady on TV got me to open my Bible again. For the first time in a long time."

I noticed Dave was being very attentive and I had the feeling that maybe Elena hadn't told him everything just yet. I was relieved that there was more to the story than someone heard that I had seen Jesus. Because that would seem like a faith built on something other than rock.

She kept going. "And I saw in the Bible that in all things God works for the good of those who love Him. And I want that hope again, Bob."

Mary's eyes were also big by this time. I asked, "Do you believe that, Elena?" It wasn't accusatory. I wanted her to believe it because it was true.

A tear leaked down her cheek. "I want to believe it," she said.

***

The taco truck started up and the exhaust blew back on us. The tires spun for just a tick before they got traction and the vehicle merged onto the road and headed away. It was time to go.

I was shaking Dave's hand when I remembered. "Dave, who's Gabriella?"

They both gawked at me. Dave was almost defensive. "What did you say?"

I looked at Mary. She waved her hand, telling me to go on.

"Well, let's try to keep this between us, but I saw Jesus again. Last night. He told me to tell you that Gabriella was fine."

Elena broke down into tears and her legs gave out. As she sank down to the gravel, Dave knelt with her. They ended up on their knees facing each other and hugging. Tears streamed down both sides of Dave's face. Elena sobbed into his shoulder.

I was a little panicked. Mary came up and took my hand. I looked at her and she had the look of confusion that I was sure my own face wore. But when Dave looked up, despite the tears, I could see a smile and happiness residing there.

"Gabriella is the name of our daughter. We never told anyone that that was what her name was going to be. We didn't even know she was going to be a girl. But she was. Our precious Gabriella."

He turned his head back against Elena's face. With one hand he stroked her black hair. Mary squeezed my hand and I looked into her eyes to find tears as well. How blessed we are when we see our God at work.

In a rush, all of a sudden James was right in our midst. He looked panicked.

"Dad, what happened? What's wrong? Why is Uncle Dave crying?"

I put my hand on his shoulder and pulled him tight against my hip. His mother put a hand on his shoulder, too.

"It's okay, Buddy," I said. "Not all tears are bad."

21

I was up early Sunday morning and headed to the church. A little quiet time before the service was to start. I checked on James and gave Mary a kiss. I don't know that she was fully awake, but that was okay.

I left my coffee sitting on the counter, however. Not how I wanted to start the workday: forgetful. It's a small town. I could have easily just turned around and went back home and got my coffee. Or I could have stopped in at McDonalds. Instead, I went for door number three: Marcos's liquor store. I'd had coffee there before and it wasn't bad. Besides, I hadn't seen Marcos since the holdup a lifetime ago.

A new face resided behind the counter. A young woman with purple hair and rings in her nose, but she seemed pleasant enough. I grabbed a Styrofoam cup and filled it, fighting to seat the lid just right. I looked around but saw no signs of Marcos.

I dug into my pocket for a couple of dollars when I got to the counter. The girl with the purple hair set down her phone and typed a couple of keys on the register. "Buck seventy-five," she said.

I handed her two ones. "Hey, how are things going this morning?"

She looked at me like I was from another planet. Her phone dinged, but she had the decency to just glance at it and then back at me. "Fine," she said, but she seemed unsure. Not if she was fine or not, but like I was up to something.

"Good. My name's Bob." I held out my hand. She looked at it for an awkward second before hesitantly extending her own hand. We shook, but she didn't offer me her name.

"Where's Marcos?" I asked.

This was a question she was better prepared to answer than trading pleasantries with a stranger. "Oh, he said he had somewhere to be this morning. Asked me to come in. And I'm kind of new, so I drew the short straw."

"Well, I'm the pastor at the church down the road. If you don't have to work one of these weekends you could swing on in."

"Sounds like a blast." She did pick up her phone then. I was dismissed.

That was okay. My mood was top notch this morning. After the wild couple of weeks, it was nice to get back to a little bit of normalcy. Not normal, though. I still had thoughts about our church and what I perceived as a bit of lethargy, but I was okay with that. Still, I was anxious to see who would show up and what the feel was. Deep down, I was a little nervous that I'd run everybody off with my antics.

No matter. Undeterred, I drove the Ranger to the church, parking in the back. It looked like another beautiful day was in store. The sun was up now and the briskness of the morning was giving way to the sun's warmth. The high temps would be hitting the area soon enough, so it was best to enjoy any briskness before it gave way to summer heat.

I opened my office and went in. I took a rag and wiped at my small window. I wanted as much sun as I could muster to get in. I plopped in my chair and took out my sermon notes and spread them out. The sermon had come easy enough once I had sat down to it yesterday evening. This was the fun part, right? The good soil. Fruit. Harvest.

We'd spent the last couple of sermons going over the soil and what we could do to cultivate that. In the process, I hoped I had tilled and weeded and cleared some of the congregation's soil. The purpose of all of that was to produce a crop. A farming community understood what a good crop meant.

Still, it felt incomplete. Like maybe I was missing just a little something. I prayed for a bit. I don't know how long. It started out very heartfelt and thankful, but I soon found my mind wandering. Was that me or was it God trying to steer my brain in other directions? Was it worries of the world or the prodding of the Lord? Thorns or fertilizer?

Somewhere in that prayer, the words that Jesus had spoken to me on that first day in my office came back. When He told me *you will have to choose your life or doing what I ask.* Had I lost my life in this last month? I had done what He'd asked, but where was I now? Had my own soil been worked over?

I shook my head and gave an amen. The sermon notes continued to mock me. I went over them again. It was a pretty decent sermon. It would be fine.

***

When the worship team was in the middle of the second song, I kind of tuned out. My seat was facing the congregation and I took in the people. The turnout was about normal. Not packed as we had been for the last month, but not sparsely populated, either. No TV crews this time. Everyone was standing and singing along and I started to feel strange.

It was very similar to the experience at the Lucifer concert, when I was certain that the Spirit was taking over everything. What I felt was this sense of love for the people in those seats. The body of Christ together to worship. My brothers and sisters in Jesus. I thought I might cry.

I took a quick note of who was there. It seemed all of the trustees were present today. Bill Jones stifled a yawn, but he was up and singing with the rest. George and Lila Liston were in their usual spot. Matthew was beside them and actually singing along. Sure, he was still wearing black, but I think that was all that his wardrobe consisted of.

I now knew where Marcos had been off to this morning: he was sitting in the third row. I had seen him before church and it turns out he had been at the revival before things had spiraled out of control. Titus had stirred something in him. He seemed uncomfortable talking about it, but I knew we'd speak soon enough. I would probably be getting more coffee from the liquor store.

He wasn't the only new face either. Sheriff McKinney from the robbery incident was there, too. And the greasy jeans guy. He was hard to recognize, because he was cleaned up a little now, but he stood tall and sang with the rest of us. He was standing next to Dave and Elena. And just behind them was Mary and James who would be going in the back with the rest of the Sunday School crowd once the music was over.

I put a hand to my face and pretended I had something in my eye. I better get it together if I was going to get up and preach. I turned and looked just at the band and tried to focus on the music and the words of worship.

But those people had experienced God through the craziness of the last four or five weeks. And I had been a part of that. Maybe I had helped to do something with their soil. To make it more receptive. Although, as I recounted the individual experiences, I noticed a pattern.

THORNS

Marcos had come not because of the multiple visits and talks I'd had with him, but because of something out of Paul's letter to Titus. And Matthew had garnered a bit of hope from my message at the concert. No particular book in that one, but all Scripture from the Bible. Romans had got him. Elena had found newfound faith also in the words of the Bible. Even Mary had been restored to me. Not by something I said, but something I'd repeated that Jesus had told me.

Maybe I hadn't done much at all. I'd just fed them what I had read in the Scripture. Like I was just a messenger. Or a plagiarist. I don't know, maybe a... sower?

The band faded into silence. Not in real life, but just in my head. I was alone with that thought. The sower. The parable of the sower. I wasn't a farmer and the soil was not my concern. I just needed to throw the Word out there and let Someone else worry about the rest.

At some point I realized that the band was now, in actuality, silent. The whole room was silent and looking at me. It was time for the sermon. I looked down in my fist and saw my notes crumpled there. They would be hard to read, but that was okay. I had a different message now.

The sower...

22

It was the best sermon I have ever preached. Top notch, fill the pews, people-swooning-in-the-aisles sort of sermon. Look out Billy Graham. Hey trustees, get ready to build a bigger sanctuary. A whole movement might be starting right here and now. Right up there with the sermon on the mount.

Okay, that may be an exaggeration. But it was good. And moving. And powerful. It was all impromptu. Off the cuff. I started with an apology of sorts. Hey gang, I've been going pretty hard lately and maybe I thought I could change the world on my own. I can't. But we know someone who does.

It felt good to get that off my plate. Like a heavy load was lifted off my shoulders. I felt lighter on my feet. I was able to look out on my congregation with only the love that Christ had placed there. I suppose that was my job, as well. Not just to sow the Word, but to love these people. I found now that I had gotten out of my own way a little bit, I could do that. At least, I could do it better than I ever had been able to before.

Sure, I stammered some and missed the point and had to backtrack. I may have gone down a rabbit trail or two, but that's what happens when you go with no notes or outlines or simply change your message right at the last minute.

We still talked about the good soil and the harvest, but I got to tell the people there that it wasn't necessarily our concern. But we had to spread the Word. God reaped the harvest.

I even started sweating up there. I was on a roll and no one fell asleep. I didn't even notice anyone look at their watch. The Spirit had ahold of me and I was just along for the ride.

My concept of time was not totally askew, however. I knew when we had probably gone long enough. I had hit the point of the message and I'd given us all something to take with us and work into our lives. It was a worshipful sermon. How they all should be.

Before the worship team came back up for the last song, I led us all in prayer. And maybe it wasn't as deeply personal as the one that had drawn Jesus into my office, but it was strong. It was heartfelt. And I didn't want it to return empty, so I left most of my words out, and put mostly His Words in.

Made in the USA
Coppell, TX
08 December 2025